1-96 1⅞ Read Very Good 11-'96
RS
a

*Young and in love, Joelle Dawson's dreams of wedded bliss are about to be challenged.*

"I suppose you're right," Joelle replied, nervously biting at her lower lip. "It's just that I love him so much. I'm so afraid something will happen to spoil it all."

"Trust in the Lord, Joelle," Daughtry advised. "He's the One Who holds the future. If it's right for you and John to marry, God will see to it that nothing else interferes."

"But what if it isn't what God wants?" Joelle questioned, suddenly realizing for the first time that perhaps there was a larger stumbling block to her happiness than she had even allowed herself to imagine.

"If it's not right, Joelle, then you certainly don't want to defy God and marry John." Joelle's panic-stricken face caused Daughtry to hurry ahead. "But I know John and I know he wouldn't have asked you to marry him, without having first asked God. He must feel quite confident about it, or he wouldn't have come this far."

D0695810

**Tracie J. Peterson** is a popular inspirational writer from Kansas. Tracie has also written eight successful **Heartsong Presents** titles under the name of Janelle Jamison. *Come Away My Love* continues Tracie's popular style of sweet western romance.

HEARTSONG PRESENTS

**Books by Janelle Jamison**
HP19—A Place to Belong
HP40—Perfect Love
HP47—Tender Journeys
HP56—A Light in the Window
HP63—The Willing Heart
HP71—Destiny's Road
HP88—Beyond Today
HP93—Iditarod Dream

**Books by Tracie J. Peterson**
HP102—If Given a Choice
HP111—A Kingdom Divided
HP116—The Heart's Calling
HP127—Forever Yours
HP140—Angel's Cause
HP164—Alas My Love
HP182—A Wing and a Prayer
HP186—Wings Like Eagles

Don't miss out on any of our super romances. Write to us at the following address for information on our newest releases and club information.

Heartsong Presents Readers' Service
P.O. Box 719
Uhrichsville, OH 44683

# Come Away My Love

*Tracie J. Peterson*

*Heartsong Presents*

Dedicated to: Don Grover with thanks
for the many hours of computer input
and output and in general, putting up
with my crisis calls. Here's your fifteen minutes of fame.

A note from the Author:
*I love to hear from my readers! You may correspond
with me by writing:*

Tracie J. Peterson
Author Relations
P.O. Box 719
Uhrichsville, OH 44683

ISBN 1-55748-924-6

**COME AWAY MY LOVE**

© 1996 by Tracie J. Peterson. All rights reserved. Except for
use in any review, the reproduction or utilization of this work in
whole or in part in any form by any electronic, mechanical, or
other means, now known or hereafter invented, is forbidden
without the permission of the publisher, Heartsong Presents,
P.O. Box 719, Uhrichsville, Ohio 44683.

All of the characters and events in this book are fictitious. Any
resemblance to actual persons, living or dead, or to actual
events is purely coincidental.

*Cover illustration by Kathy Arbuckle*

PRINTED IN THE U.S.A.

## *one*

"There it goes again," the pilot yelled over the roar of the Jenny's engine. "Don't tell me you didn't hear it that time, Flipflop." The young man in grease-smeared khaki shrugged his shoulders.

Lieutenant John Monroe, the Jenny's pilot, switched off the engine and leaped to the ground as though he might take issue with the confused private. Flipflop, as he was affectionately called because of his nervous stomach at flight time, backed up defensively.

"I mean it, Preacher, I didn't hear it missing out!"

John stopped short and offered a grin. "Then you take her up."

The private smiled back. He knew John's words were said in jest only. There was not a pilot around who would let another man take up his lady, if he were able to fly her himself.

"I'll help you take the engine apart again," Flipflop offered.

"Naw," John said and tossed aside his leather cap and goggles. "Go get some grub. I'll stay here and see if I can't figure out which cylinder it is. Say, where's that worthless brother of mine?"

Flipflop shrugged. "Last time I saw J.D., I mean Sergeant Monroe, he was heading to the mess. You want me to send him out here?"

John shook his head. "No, go on. J.D.'s no doubt managed to finagle a pass into town. I won't have him feeling obligated to help me here." The private shrugged again and gratefully headed to the mess tent.

John gave the Curtiss Jenny a determined stare. "You are sure one cantankerous lady today," he muttered. At twenty-five, John had realized his dream of flying. It was a young dream, just like the art itself. But nevertheless, it was in his blood, and John could think of nothing that gave him more enjoyment and pleasure than soaring overhead, master of the Jenny.

He laughed at that thought. "Some master. I can't even figure out what's wrong with you. Why don't you talk to me, honey?"

The biplane sat in smug silence. If she were a flesh-and-blood woman, the cold-shouldered indifference could not have been more simply stated. But she was not a woman, not in the sense of flesh and blood, and she certainly was not a lady.

Yet, John could not help but grin at her in the same affectionate manner that he would have his beloved Joelle. Ah, Joelle, he thought. He could see her dark eyes blazing with the same love and excitement he felt.

"Pity the woman who shares a man with his plane." Those famed words from John's good friend and commander, Major Bob Camstead, were followed up with a haunting prediction: "She'll always run a close second."

But John did not think so. He considered Joelle Dawson to rank right up there with his aggravating Jenny. The only problem was, would Joelle see it the same way?

John heard the unmistakable approach of another Jenny overhead and stared out wistfully to where she was. There was absolutely nothing like it, he thought. John watched on in silence as the pilot cut back the engine and bounced to a rough landing with the Jenny's tail skid absorbing most of the impact.

"Flying up there gives a man a great belief in the reality of God," Bob Camstead had once told him. "But landings were sure to get you religious in a quick way, if you weren't already set in your thoughts."

John smiled and went to work on the engine. He had no doubt about the existence of God, nor of the love and peace that could be found when an obedient heart sought His way. Landing Jennys on rocky desert strips had not given John religion, but it had kept him regular in his prayer life.

❧

It was late that night when John finally managed to locate the problem with the engine. After a quick bite of food and a shower, John sat down to write to Joelle. While sweating over the engine, he had made up his mind that he was going to ask her to be his wife. Picking up his pencil, he wondered how he should go about it.

He started to write, then shook his head and discarded the piece of paper and picked up a clean sheet. Maybe she would think it was too soon. What if he had misunderstood her feelings? No, he reasoned, that was not possible. He put the pencil down and thought for a moment. It had to be just right.

The well-worn Bible that he had brought with him to army life sat on his bed. It had been his habit to make it the first thing he read when he woke up in the morning and the last thing he saw before going to sleep at night. Picking it up, John began to leaf through the pages.

❧

Joelle Dawson fairly danced through the kitchen of Piñon Canyon Ranch. Her tiny frame seemed as light as air and her face was radiant in its joy.

Joelle's sister-in-law, Daughtry, rolled her eyes and suppressed a giggle. "John must have written another letter," she mused to her mother, Maggie Lucas.

Maggie watched the dark-eyed Joelle float from the room into the hallway. "She's completely gone over him, isn't she?" Maggie laughed then looked back to her daughter. "Of course, you are just as bad, oh daughter-of-mine."

"I beg your pardon?" Daughtry feigned indignation.

"Oh, don't play ingénue with me, Daughtry Dawson. You still get gaga every time Joelle's brother comes waltzing through the door. A body might think that Nicholas Dawson hung the stars and the moon in the sky."

"I'm no worse than you are about Daddy," Daughtry countered. "I've seen the way you run to the mirror and check to make sure you look your best when you hear him coming up the walk." Maggie thought to deny it, but the look on her face caused Daughtry to laugh and Maggie could not help but join her.

Joelle could hear the two women giggling like schoolgirls as she moved away from the main section of the ranch house and down the west wing. Here, the Lucases had kindly provided her a room to live in when their daughter, Daughtry, and son-in-law, Nick, had come to the ranch to anticipate the birth of their second child. Joelle was a kind of tag-along who had happily lived the last few months on Nick and Daughtry's ranch. The youngest of her family, Joelle had come to stay on with her brother in order to help care for Kent, their firstborn, and keep house for Daughtry.

At least that is what she had told her mother and father when she had pleaded to be allowed to do the deed. They had had little idea that she saw this as the best way to position herself close to the man she would come to love.

Joelle had met John Monroe at the Lucas's Christmas party, just two years earlier. He was not the kind of guy who caught everyone's eye when he walked into the room, but when Joelle first caught sight of him, she had immediately felt her heart skip a beat. He was a half-foot taller than she, with sandy blond hair and the most stunning blue eyes she had ever seen in her life.

That evening had been the most perfect one she had ever known. Although there had been many other men trying to get Joelle's attention that night, she had enjoyed talking to John the most. Daughtry alone had five brothers and John had a younger brother who was not to be outdone by his sibling. There was also another young man, John's cousin, Sam, but no one else mattered much after she had met John. By the time the party was over, Joelle knew that John Monroe was the man she intended to marry.

Clutching the latest letter from her beloved John, Joelle dreamily closed the door behind her as she sought her privacy. Unable to contain her excitement any longer, she tore open the envelope and read the words of Song of Solomon 2:10-11.

> *"My beloved spake, and said unto me, Rise up, my love, my fair one, and come away. For, lo, the winter is past, the rain is over and gone."*

Joelle loved John's romantic notions and the way he used Scripture to court her. Her own faith in God was still a tender mystery to her, but John's was robust and invigorating. She found strength in it. She continued to read.

> *My beloved Joelle,*
> *I would like to like to be at your side*
> *when you read these words, but the army*
> *doesn't care how or when a man proposes his*
> *love. They only care that when duty calls, I*
> *answer and that I do it in double-time.*

Joelle felt her heart beat faster. This was the letter for which she had been waiting. After what had seemed an eternity of time, Joelle knew herself to be hopelessly in love with the handsome army lieutenant and she could only hope he felt the same. She closed her eyes, savoring the letter, wanting to make the moment last as long as possible.

She pictured in her mind John's tousled, blond hair blowing across his forehead and falling haphazardly across his sky blue eyes. She had not seen him in person since his sister, Angeline, had married Daughtry's brother, Gavin Lucas. That was nearly three months ago, not that it mattered. She could still hear his voice, soft against her ear. . . still see him waving goodbye from the cockpit of his biplane.

"Oh, John," she whispered his name as praise and turned her eyes back to the paper in hand.

> *Once, it was only a dream of mine that I*
> *might find a woman to love. A woman with*

> *whom I could plan a future. You, Joelle, are*
> *that woman. I can't imagine life without you*
> *and every day that passes without knowing*
> *that you officially belong to me, grieves me*
> *as surely as anything has ever grieved me. I*
> *know this lacks the flowers and candlelight*
> *that you deserve, but, Joelle, I am hopelessly*
> *in love with you and. . . .*

Joelle paused to take a deep breath before she continued reading.

> *ask, with humble, loving heart, that you*
> *would consent to be my wife.*

Joelle let out a scream of delight without even being consciously aware of what she had done. The sound of hurried footsteps in the hallway soon brought Maggie through the doorway, followed by the slower moving Daughtry.

"What is it, Joelle?" Maggie questioned in worried overtones. "Are you hurt?"

Joelle clutched the letter to her breast. She shook her head and breathlessly replied, "He's asked me to marry him!"

Daughtry leaned against the door and smiled. "Is that all?"

The three women were soon embracing one another joyously. Joelle was the first to pull away. She could not stand still for very long and Maggie laughed at the way the petite woman flitted from one corner of the room to the other.

"I'm so happy, I shall cry," Joelle said, the emotion heavy in her voice. "Oh, Daughtry, Maggie, this is exactly what

I've hoped and prayed for."

"I can't imagine a finer wife for John," Maggie stated, meaning every word.

"Or a better husband for Joelle," Daughtry added. "I certainly wouldn't wish any of my brothers on her."

"Oh, hush," Maggie said, waggling a finger at her daughter. "You have excellent brothers and what with Gavin married to John's little sister, I have only four others to marry off."

"Good luck," Daughtry continued her mock harangue. "You're going to have to send away for wives. The women around here know them too well to be taken in by that Lucas charm."

All three women laughed, but each knew the merriment was not credited to Daughtry's words. It was clearly Joelle's joyous expectation of marriage to John.

"We should go right away and tell Lillie," Maggie suggested, thinking of the woman who was her lifelong best friend and John's mother. "No doubt John will write to his folks when he gets a chance, but a mother likes to know these things right away and Lillie won't be any exception."

Joelle sobered a bit. "Do you think she'll approve? She won't think it rushed, will she?"

"John's mother is as romantic as the next woman," Maggie said, reaching out to smooth back a strand of Joelle's dark hair from her face. "Besides, I think Lillie already has a good idea of what John's intending to do."

"Honestly?" Joelle's eyes were wide in anticipation of Maggie's response.

"She told me, not two days ago, that she thought John was quite sweet on you," Maggie replied. "In fact, she commented that knowing John's penchants for moving right ahead with things and his rather romantic outlook on life, that she expected to have a daughter-in-law by spring."

"Oh, Maggie!" Joelle gasped. "That's wonderful. Then you think she really won't mind? I mean, I know John will want to get married right away."

"I don't think she'll mind at all. Why don't you get a letter of acceptance off to him and when you're finished, we can ride into town together and post it and then go see Lillie."

Joelle threw herself into Maggie's arms. "I don't know how to thank you. You've all been so kind and good to me."

"No thanks are necessary," Maggie said, giving Joelle a hug. "You've been a blessing to Daughtry and that in turn has blessed me. What with the way Kent runs around here like a wild banshee—"

"Speaking of my son," Daughtry said with a sudden worried tone, "I'd better locate him and see what mischief he's gotten himself into."

"Don't worry about it," Joelle said, pulling away from Maggie. "When Jordy brought me this letter, I traded him Kent."

Daughtry grinned. "That ought to teach my baby brother to go fetching mail for moon-eyed young ladies."

"I am not moon-eyed," Joelle protested, but very weakly. "I'm in love! And, I'm getting married!"

About fifteen minutes later, Joelle appeared in the kitchen, her readied response in hand. Maggie was nowhere to be seen, but Daughtry was vigorously kneading down bread dough. Glancing up, Daughtry could not help but smile. Joelle had apparently not only written the letter, but had also changed her clothes and rearranged her hair.

"Wanting to make a good impression on your future

mother-in-law, I see?" Daughtry teased.

"Oh, Dotty," Joelle answered, staring down at her outfit, "do I look perfectly awful?"

"Not at all. I think you look very fit. Mother is having the buggy brought around. I don't know why Daddy won't just get a car and make it easier on all of us."

Joelle wriggled her noise. "They smell funny, anyway."

"So do horses," Daughtry laughed.

"I guess that's so. But truly, do you think I look all right? I was going to wear the blue serge but it looked too stuffy. Then I tried on my green skirt with the plum piping, but it just didn't seem right, either."

Daughtry left her bread, wiping her hands as she came to where Joelle stood. "Turn around and let me see." She motioned with her hand and Joelle pirouetted in slow motion. Joelle had finally settled on a lavender print dress. "Yes, you look just fine. That dress really sets off your figure."

"What about my hair?" Joelle questioned, her hand going up to readjust her hat. It was a wide-brimmed straw affair with a lavender scarf to tie it smartly to her head. "Does this hat seem a bit too much?"

"Don't all hats, these days?" Daughtry questioned lightly. "Nick says if they get any larger we can just turn them over and use them as laundry baskets."

Joelle looked at her sister-in-law in horror. "Does it look that bad?"

Daughtry laughed. "The hat is fine. You hair is perfect. Your face is free of smudges and dirt, although given the ride into Bandelero, it won't take long to rectify that. Joelle, relax. You know Lillie Monroe adores you. She'll want only the very best for her son and for you."

"I suppose you're right," Joelle replied, nervously biting at her lower lip. "It's just that I love him so much. I'm so afraid something will happen to spoil it all."

"Trust in the Lord, Joelle," Daughtry advised. "He's the One Who holds the future. If it's right for you and John to marry, God will see to it that nothing else interferes."

"But what if it isn't what God wants?" Joelle questioned, suddenly realizing for the first time that perhaps there was a larger stumbling block to her happiness than she had even allowed herself to imagine.

"If it's not right, Joelle, then you certainly don't want to defy God and marry John." Joelle's panic-stricken face caused Daughtry to hurry ahead. "But I know John and I know he wouldn't have asked you to marry him, without having first asked God. He must feel quite confident about it, or he wouldn't have come this far."

Joelle's smile was back in place. "Of course, you're right! John would never propose marriage without feeling sure that God was leading him in this. All right, Daughtry. I shan't worry another moment about Lillie. I know God will see to the entire matter. I just know it!"

❧

John was up to his elbows in grease when Flipflop approached him with Joelle's letter. The Jenny was causing him problems again, though in all honesty it was not her fault. The army was experimenting with the loads she could carried. They continued to add and take away various items from the plane, until John was not all that certain if the engine had been removed by direct order of his superiors.

"You got a letter, Preacher," Flipflop said with a grin. "I think it's the one you've been waiting for."

John quickly picked up a rag and wiped his hands. His

face was smudged from the oil and his hair, which was due for a trimming anyway, had taken on a darker appearance from his time spent over and inside, the Jenny's V-8 engine.

"Give it here," John said, throwing the rag down.

"You wanna be alone, Preach?" Flipflop asked hesitantly. The tone in his voice left little doubt that he hoped to be a part of the missive.

"Naw," John said, trying to keep his voice even. "Might as well stay. You've earned it just having to work with me these last few days.

Flipflop smiled his gratitude and matched the way John sucked in his breath as the top of the envelope gave way. Unable to slow his fingers, John tore at the folds of the letter until it opened to his scrutiny.

> *"His mouth is most sweet: yea, he is altogether lovely. This is my beloved, and this is my friend. . . ."* *The words of Song of Solomon 5:16 reminded me of you, John, and I could scarcely contain my joy when I received your marriage proposal. I will most happily rise up and come away, my love. I am yours, now and forever, and joyfully I will become your wife at the first possible moment.*
>
> *Your beloved Joelle*

John gave out a whoop that was loud enough to be heard, not only across the airfield, but throughout all of El Paso, as well. "She said yes! She's gonna marry me, Flipflop!" John kissed the single-page letter and let out another yell. "She said yes!"

## two

January brought them mild and pleasant conditions. Joelle enjoyed a continuous flow of mail from John, as well as a new-found friendship in her soon-to-be mother-in-law, Lillie Monroe.

"I can't believe this weather!" Lillie exclaimed coming into the house from outside. "I haven't worn a coat all week and today I'm even tempted to roll up these long sleeves, but Dan would skin me alive if he caught me." Although Lillie teased as though her husband was a harsh man, Joelle had witnessed the deep love they held for each other.

Joelle glanced up from the receiving blanket she was embroidering for Daughtry's new baby. "I keep thinking how wonderful it would be if only John and I could get married now. Why, we could even have our wedding outside, like Angeline and Gavin did last fall.

Lillie nodded, a faint smile crossing her lips at the memory of her youngest child's wedding. She had seen very little of Angeline or Gavin since their marriage. Her smile broadened at the thought of the newlyweds.

"What?" Joelle questioned, catching Lillie's expression.

Lillie shook her head. "It's nothing really. I was just thinking how little I've seen of Angeline since she got married. Maggie says that Gavin is pretty scarce, too, and except for working with his father, she doesn't believe he ever leaves Angeline's side."

"I feel the same way about John," Joelle confessed.

"I hate the separation and I'd give just about anything if he were here. I'd pray for God to find a way to muster John out of the army, but I know how much he loves flying." There was an unexpected heaviness in Joelle's voice. "I think it will be hard being an army wife. I can't imagine getting married, only to have to send him off for long separations."

Lillie sat down across from Joelle and picked up her own sewing. "I know. I wish neither one of the boys had run off and joined up the way they did. I'm so afraid we'll be drawn into the war in Europe. Every day we seem to get that much closer to choosing sides. Of course," Lillie paused, "there is really no contest in that. We can't possibly support the way Germany has acted. Daniel tells me that there is a great deal of propaganda, some of it true, some of it exaggerated, but nonetheless, it doesn't come out in favor of Germany."

"I saw one of the posters at the post office," Joelle confessed.

"The one with the poor little children asleep in their beds with the outline of the Hun soldiers overshadowing them?" Lillie questioned.

"Yes," Joelle replied with a shudder. She took several tiny stitches and put the blanket down. "How can people be so cruel to children?"

"I haven't a clue. I wish I could extend the same cruelty to those who dish it out, but Daniel says we must pray for even the cruelest of Germany's soldiers. God doesn't want our anger to turn into something just as ugly. Revenge belongs to God."

"I suppose he's right," Joelle said with a wistful look to the window beyond Lillie. "Still, it would seem justified. I mean God can't possibly expect folks to allow such horrors to go unchecked."

Lillie nodded with a smile. "I feel exactly like you do, Joelle. We're going to get along just fine."

Joelle beamed, "Oh, by the way, I forgot to thank you for having me over today. I cherish our visits." She paused for a moment to take in her soon-to-be mother-in-law. Lillie Monroe was a very stylish woman. She wore her blond hair in a short, yet feminine bob. There was just a bit of silver amidst the honey gold that betrayed her middle age. The thing that fascinated Joelle most, however, was Lillie's seeming perfection. She was good at everything she touched and everyone in Bandelero loved her.

Joelle suddenly felt insecure again. " I was so afraid you wouldn't want me for a daughter-in-law," she confessed.

With a surprised look on her face, Lillie looked up from her work. Her eyes softened as she considered the young woman across the table. "I feel quite blessed to have such a lovely young woman join my family," Lillie said in reply. "I sincerely mean that, Joelle. I'm pleased with John's choice for a wife. He's a sound young man with a heart for God. If he's prayed about this and sought the Lord's guidance, which I'm sure he has, who am I to interfere?"

"Not all mother-in-laws would feel that way," Joelle said with a grin. "Maggie told me the other day that her son, Dolan, got a bit of a cold shoulder from Judy Miller's mother. It seems that even though Dolan's family has plenty of wealth, Dolan himself hasn't proved a thing regarding how he would support a wife. Poor Dolan," Joelle laughed, "he wasn't even that far along in thinking, but Mrs. Miller sure gave him an earful."

"I think it's well for a parent, a mother of a daughter in this case, to know what the prospective husband of her child plans to do with his life. After all, his life is no longer his own. He is suddenly a very important part of another human being. A human being on whom you, as a parent, have spent a great deal of time and energy to grow to adulthood."

"That does seem reasonable," Joelle agreed. "So how come you haven't asked me what I plan to do with my life?"

Lillie laughed. "Because I don't have to. You plan to love my son with all your heart. It couldn't be any clearer."

Joelle blushed. "I can't imagine not loving him, Lillie. He's so important to me."

"I know. I'm not so old that I can't remember what it felt like to fall in love."

Joelle looked rather surprised. "You mean you aren't still in love?"

Lillie paused for a moment to consider her answer. "In love, no." Joelle looked crestfallen. "But I deeply and completely love my husband. You see, to me, falling in love is like jumping into a cool pond on a hot day. It's shocking and exhilarating at first, then as you become accustomed to it, you find it more and more comfortable, even ordinary."

"My love for John could never be ordinary," Joelle protested.

"Good, I'm glad to hear it. You'll do well in marriage if you work toward that end. It's when things become routine and ordinary that you can get off track," Lillie replied, leaning back in her chair. "But just like swimming in a pond, Joelle, you dare not take it for granted. When you take the water for granted, you drown. The minute you take love for granted, you lose something very precious. And, it's extremely hard to get it back."

"I'll remember that," Joelle said, picking up her sewing again.

Lillie started to say something in reply when a knock at the door distracted her thoughts. "I wonder who's injured themselves now?"

Joelle found life at the Monroe house more than a little bit interesting. Daniel Monroe was one of only two doctors in the entire area surrounding Bandelero. And, given the fact that he had been the only doctor for over twenty years, people were still partial to his kind of doctoring. It was nothing for Lillie and Dan to see a steady stream of cut fingers, infected wounds, and hacking coughs, all in the same day. Of course, there were those times when the ailments were much more serious.

It took only a moment for Lillie to return, but when she did her face was ashen and in her hand was the unmistakable cause.

"A telegram?" Joelle questioned, wondering at Lillie's worried expression. When their eyes met, Joelle felt her breath catch.

"It's from the army." The words lingered in the air for an eternity before Lillie added, "John's been in an accident."

"No!" Joelle abandoned her sewing and crossed the room to Lillie. "No, it can't be true. He's not. . .? He isn't. . .?" She could not ask the question.

"No, he isn't dead. At least not yet. Joelle, we have to send for Dan. John's going to need him. We have to go to him right away." Joelle worried that Lillie might faint and so she gently led her to the chair.

"I'll get him myself," Joelle said and pulled her shawl

around her shoulders. "Where did he go this morning?"

Lillie tried in vain to remember. "I don't know. I think he had calls to make at Mrs. Brown's and maybe Joe Perkum's."

"I'll go to Mrs. Brown's house first," Joelle said. "Will you be all right here alone?"

"I'll be fine, Joelle. Just get Dan. Please, just bring Dan home."

❧

Joelle raced down the sandy dirt street outside the Monroe house. She was grateful that she had spent so much time with Maggie and Daughtry in Bandelero. She was rapidly learning her way around and now was confident in her mission to locate Dr. Dan.

"Oh, God," Joelle breathed, completely unaware of the tears that streamed down her face. "Please, God." It was all that she could say, yet it made her feel better.

A quick visit to the Brown's red-brick residence revealed that Dan had been there earlier, but had moved on to tend to another patient. Mrs. Brown had the presence of mind to pick up the telephone and ask the operator if she knew where Dr. Dan had taken himself.

"He's over at Morely Davis's place," the operator replied. "He just checked in with me not five minutes ago."

"Thank you, Sarah," Mrs. Brown said, then turned to Joelle. "He's with Morely Davis. Do you know where that is?"

"I don't think so," Joelle replied, her voice near to a sob.

The older woman nodded sympathetically, wondering at the young woman's dilemma, but uncharacteristically she kept her questions to herself. "You go past the bank and turn down the alley. You'll come to Second Street and then turn left. Morely's is behind the Red Dog Saloon."

"Thank you, Mrs. Brown," Joelle barely had the presence of mind to mutter. She quickly took off running, hiking her long brown skirt higher to accommodate her leggy strides.

"Dan! Dr. Dan!" Joelle yelled, even before coming to Morely's door. Several passing residents of Bandelero paused to consider her cries, waiting and watching to see what the trouble might be. In a town the size of Bandelero, one family's troubles were quickly shared by all.

Just as Joelle reached out to pound against Morely's door, Daniel himself opened the door and stepped outside. He was so like John in appearance, that seeing him caused Joelle's tears to start anew.

"Joelle! What is it, honey? What's wrong?"

"Oh, Dan!" she exclaimed breathlessly. "You have to come home."

"Is Lillie hurt?" Dan's face drained of color.

"No," Joelle's voice broke. "It's John. He's been in an accident. Lillie says you have to come home. Please, Dan." She reached up as if she might have to drag him back to the house.

There was no need to beg. Dan quickly finished with Morley, retrieved his bag, and joined Joelle in the street. "Come on," he said, putting his arm around the trembling young woman. "We'll go home and find out what's to be done."

Joelle nodded, grateful for Dan's gesture. "I want to go with you." She stated the words so quietly that she wondered if Dan had even heard them.

"Of course," he replied with a tender smile. "I wouldn't dream of going to John without taking you with us."

꙾

After several telephone calls, Dan was able to ascertain that John had crashed his Jenny while testing flight loads west of El Paso. The rest of the details were sketchy, at best. All they knew for sure was that he was in the hospital in Columbus, New Mexico and it would take the better part of a day and night to get to him.

By evening, the Monroes, with Joelle in tow, were on the train headed to Santa Fe. From there they would catch a train on the Santa Fe main line and head south to Columbus.

For Joelle, it seemed that forever separated her from her beloved. She paced the train until the steward and, finally, the conductor himself, pleaded with Dan to keep her seated.

Around midnight, Joelle fell into a fitful sleep. She saw John in his biplane, circling overhead. She heard him trying to shout something above the roar of the Jenny's engine, but she could not make it out.

"What are you saying, John? I can't hear you!" she cried out in her dream.

John smiled down at her and the engine fell silent. "Rise up my love, my fair one, and come away."

Joelle stirred, crying in her sleep. Dan wished silently that he could comfort her. Staring down at his wife, equally as restless but nestled against his comforting arm, Dan wondered at what they would find when they reached Columbus. Had John died already?

Rubbing his weary eyes, Dan thought back to his conversation with the army doctor in Columbus. Later, he had not shared the full details with Lillie, for fear that her own knowledge of medicine would leave her feeling hopeless.

John had sustained severe breaks in his leg and back. It was even possible that the spinal cord had been severed, but the doctor was unsure. Casts had been applied both to the leg and to the trunk of John's body. The doctor hesitated to say anything more. All he could tell Dan for certain was that John was conscious and had no feeling from the waist down. Perhaps, mercifully so, Dan reasoned and issued a prayer on behalf of his son.

The foreign scenery beyond the windows of the train held little interest to Joelle or the Monroes. There were vast stretches of desert land where the only thing to break the monotony was the cactus. At each and every small town Joelle perked up when the train began to slow. Always she hoped and prayed that they had reached their destination and that the conductor would announce Columbus. Time after time this was not the case and the conductor had come to merely shake his head at Joelle, before even announcing to the other passengers the town in which they were about to stop.

When the small border town of Columbus finally did come into view, Joelle felt suddenly afraid. What if John had been too weak to survive? What if while they were traveling, he had died and the army had buried him? Tears came to her eyes. Would she ever see him again?

"Come on, now," Dan said, reaching out to squeeze Joelle's hand. "Everything will be all right."

Joelle nodded. "I want to believe that."

"Good," Dan said softly. Then looking from Joelle to Lillie and back again, he added, "then believe it. God has

everything under His watchful eye. He controls our desti-
nies and He certainly controls John's." The women nodded, but said nothing and Dan was grateful for their silence.

∿

"We've given him the best facilities available," the army
doctor was saying. "We still know very little about his condition, but at least he is conscious. Coherent, too. In fact I
must warn you he's easily agitated and can be difficult."

Lillie smiled her first smile in days. "I've lived with him
long enough to know that side of him, Doctor. Have no
fear, I've seen my son's temper on more than one occasion.
I'm just grateful he's alive and capable of throwing his fits."

The doctor countered her smile. "Strange guy, your son,
if you'll pardon my saying so. He never curses, although
he's been in a great deal of pain."

"Pain?" Dan asked. "Has he regained feeling in his legs?"
Lillie and Joelle both looked up with a start.

The doctor shook his head. "No, but he has other injuries
that are causing him discomfort. He rants and raves at all
of us without regard to rank or duty. He's entitled, though.
It is a miracle that he lived through that crash. There was
little left of his plane."

Lillie cringed. "He's paralyzed?"

"I'm afraid so," the army doctor replied, hesitating only
long enough to glance at Dan. "We don't know if it's permanent or not. Only time will tell."

"I see," Lillie murmured, throwing an accusing look at
her husband. "And you knew this and didn't tell me?"

"Look, Lillie, I didn't want to worry you more than you
already were. You know almost as much about medicine as
I do and I knew you'd understand the full implications."

"Which are what?" Joelle interrupted.

All three turned to take in the small woman who looked more like a frightened urchin than anything else. Joelle did not like the look they gave her.

"What does it mean? You have to tell me!" she insisted in a barely audible voice. Her nerves were raw from the strain.

Dan reached out and touched her gently on the shoulder. "John may have severed his spinal cord in the accident. We don't know a great deal at this point, so speculating won't help anyone. It may just be that the tissue around the spine is swollen, if not. . . well. . ."

"What happens if the cord is severed?" Joelle insisted.

Dan looked helplessly to Lillie and then to his colleague. "It means that John would never walk again."

## three

Joelle took the news with surprising grace. "But John is alive, right?" She again looked to the three faces that stared back at her.

"Yes, he is," the doctor assured her. "And I haven't any reason to believe he won't pull through. He's already passed through some of the most critical checkpoints. He survived the casting, which is always a delicate matter. However, I can't begin to give you an accurate prognosis of his future condition."

Joelle squared her shoulders. "The future's in God's hands. What I want to know is how I can help the present."

The doctor nodded. "I understand. If you'll give me a moment with John, I want to make sure he's up to this visit."

He left quickly and Dan smiled down at his son's fiancée. "That's the spirit, Joelle."

"I want to see him," Joelle said without returning Dan's smile. "But," she added with thoughtfulness, "I understand that you and Lillie should see him first. I'll wait until you call for me."

Dan shook his head. "No, you'll come with us. You're an important part of John's life. He wants to build his future with you and I think you should be there."

Lillie reached out and squeezed Joelle's arm supportively. "That's right. We're in this together. If anything will see John through this accident, it will be the three of us, working as a team. Agreed?"

Joelle now smiled. "Agreed."

"Agreed, with one exception," Dan replied. "God's going to head up the effort or it won't work at all."

"Of course," Lillie and Joelle said in unison.

The doctor returned and motioned them to follow. Joelle tried to brace herself for the worst, without having any idea what the worst might be. She tried to pray, but found her lips unable to form words. Instead, she cried out with her heart and soul, feeling that her efforts were so very inadequate.

Dan and Lillie entered the room after the doctor, with Joelle following closely behind them. She could not see John yet, but heard Lillie exclaim his name and rush to his bedside.

"How dare you crash your plane!" Lillie teased to keep herself from tears.

John's bruised and battered face took in the sight of his mother's worried assessment. "I guess life just wasn't exciting enough," he replied. He was lying flat on the bed in his plaster-of-paris jacket and could not see anything past his mother and father. "You beat a path down here fast enough. You fly?"

"You won't get me up in one of those contraptions," Lillie stated flatly.

"Probably won't get me up in one again, either," John said with a bitter edge to his voice.

"You've certainly got your work cut out for you, Son," Dan said, his physician's eye sizing up the patient before him. He leaned over to better observe a particularly nasty cut on John's jaw. "Looks like they've put in about ten stitches here."

"Felt more like fifty," John declared. "I suppose maybe I should be grateful that I can't feel my legs. Doc said the one was pretty bad off. They spent a great deal of time putting me back together, or so I'm told. All I know is one minute I was in the cockpit and the next I was wearing this suit of armor."

Dan chuckled and straightened up. "I'm sure it gives you cause for frustration."

"You've got that right," John replied. "Eating is a real trick and I won't even go into detail on the process for relieving myself."

"No need to," Dan said with a nod. "I'm very familiar with catheters and even more so with bladder infections. Cystitis wouldn't help you one bit, so just be grateful for what they can do. We're going to see to it that you get back on your feet so that you won't need any of this."

"That'll be a good trick," John said, seeming to take on a completely new personality. "In fact, I'd say it might very well be impossible." The bitterness was even more evident.

"Impossible?" Lillie questioned. "I can't believe that word even came from your lips, John Monroe."

John turned his face aside, unwilling to deal with the matter. "How did Joelle take the news?" he questioned instead.

"Why don't you ask her yourself?" Dan said and reached around to pull Joelle in front of him.

It was Joelle's first chance to see John and although she wanted to cry out from the sight of her beloved with his blackened eyes still swollen and his face full of cuts, she smiled instead. "You look awful," she said as lightly as she could manage.

John stared at her for a moment as if seeing a ghost. "Get her out of here! How dare you bring her!" His voice was raised in anger, while his stony stare went past Joelle to his father. "Get her out!"

"Calm down, John," Dan said, putting supportive hands to Joelle's shoulders. "You asked this woman to be your wife. When you marry it's for sickness and health, the good with the bad. Don't you think she's strong enough to walk with you through this?"

John met Joelle's eyes unwillingly. Her face was ashen from his outburst and her eyes were rimmed with tears. Tears that he had caused. How many more would there be before it was all said and done?

"I know she's strong, but she didn't ask for this," John replied through clenched teeth.

"You didn't, either," Joelle said, breaking her silence.

"I controlled the situation," John answered. "I climbed into the plane, knowing that I was taking a risk. I had complete control and I made my choice. A pilot knows these things are always a step behind him. My time came just as I always knew it might. You can't be expected to share this, Joelle. It's too much to ask of anyone."

"But I'm not just anyone," Joelle protested and took a step toward John. "I'm going to be your wife and you are going to be my husband. My place is at your side and that is where I'm going to stay."

John shook his head. "No. You didn't know what you were doing. You didn't know this would happen. You have to go back home and forget about us, Joelle. I release you from your obligation." There were tears in his eyes, but he refused to look away from the beautiful woman at his side. He needed to remember her face, her love. It was all he had now.

Joelle put her hands on her hips to keep from burying her face in them. She stared in silence for a heartbeat, then turned to leave, surprising everyone in the room. Dan and Lillie stepped aside to let Joelle pass, but she stopped instead and turned back to John.

"You are a coward, John Monroe, but I love you all the same and," she said with a smile that betrayed her determination, "I do not release you from your obligation to marry me and until you're able to do something about it, I will continue to consider myself your bride-to-be."

She stalked from the room leaving John to stare after her in mute silence, while Lillie and Daniel broke into laughter.

"I guess she told you," Dan finally said. "You've got your hands full with that one."

"I've got nothing of the kind. This isn't a game. Dad, you've got to put her right back on the train and send her home."

"I'd like to see you try that," Lillie replied. "You apparently think Joelle will just walk away now that you are less than the object of perfection you once considered yourself to be."

"I never considered myself to be perfect!" John exclaimed, surprised at his mother's words.

"Then what's the problem?" Lillie's voice softened and she took a seat beside her son. "Would you leave Joelle if this had happened to her instead of you?"

"Of course not," John declared, "but it didn't happen to her. It happened to me. I can't marry a woman if I can't support her and I certainly can't support her while I'm on my back."

"All the more reason to get up off your back," Dan said, coming to stand beside his wife.

"The doctor said he couldn't guarantee that that would ever happen."

"I don't recall life ever coming with guarantees," Dan answered. "Leastwise, not the kind of guarantees you're looking for. Son, before you give up on a matter, you've got to at least try."

"I can't," John said in complete dejection.

"Can't never did anything," Dan said in a firm tone.

"You've said that to me since I was five years old." John's voice was changing from one of self-pity to anger. "I hated it then and I hate it now."

"It usually worked, though," Lillie remarked. "You'd storm off chanting, 'Can't never did anything! Can't never did anything! I sure wish "Can't" were here right now so I could punch him square in the nose!'" Lillie reached out to touch her son's cheek. "Remember?"

John's anger melted in view of his mother's smile. "I remember and I'd still like to give him a good one."

"Looks like he snuck up and gave you one instead," Dan said simply.

"You got that right," John grimaced as a flash of pain streaked across his head. "I don't want to deal with it right now."

"I know," Lillie sat and patted his hand. "But I also know you're going to have to quit feeling sorry for yourself. The doctor says that despite the back injury, you're in pretty good shape. The bones in your leg and back will heal and the swelling will go down. From there, we'll see what we can work with and," Lillie said with a new determination, "we'll make the best of what we have and trust God to provide the rest."

"That's asking a lot, Mom."

Lillie cocked her head to one side. "Why do you say that?"

"I don't think God much cares to provide me with anything," John answered. "I said some things that I shouldn't have when I found out about my back."

"God knows what kind of grief you were under, John. I'm sure He'll forgive you for what you said."

"He might," John replied, turning away from his mother's eyes, "if I were inclined to take them back."

❧

In the meantime, Joelle found her way outside the hospital and paced a portion of the sandy street while waiting for Daniel and Lillie to finish their visit with John. She was angry, but more than this, she was hurt. Hurt that John would push her away when he needed her so much.

"He's doesn't even know what he's saying," Joelle muttered. "He's so mad at having his wings clipped that he doesn't even know what he's saying." Then her own words rang back in her ears. Joelle stopped and stared back at the hospital.

"He doesn't know," she whispered. "He truly doesn't know." The words made her feel instantly better. Everyone said things they did not mean when they were angry or shocked. John was certainly no exception.

The revelation made Joelle's heart feel lighter. She would

just wait him out, she thought silently. It was not like he could get up from the bed and make her go home. She was a grown woman, entitled to make her own choices, and her choice was to stay put and help the man she loved.

When Dan and Lillie appeared on the street, their faces gave away grave concern. Joelle quickly joined them, wanting and needing to know what had transpired after her exit.

"He's angry, Joelle. You have to forgive him," Lillie said, pulling the younger woman to her supportively.

"I know. People say a great many things they don't mean when they're mad. I'm sure John will come around in time."

"That's a good attitude to have," Dan said, studying her face. "It's not going to be easy, however, and you must be ready for him to say a great many more things before it's all said and done."

"I kind of figured that," Joelle admitted. "But John has never seen me with my dander up. Papa used to say that had I been born first, the other three might never have arrived. I can deal with John's temper and his angry words, now that I know where they're coming from."

"And just where might that be?" Dan asked, wondering at Joelle's reasoning.

"His pain, of course." Her dark eyes turned upward to meet Dan's.

"His wounds will heal and the pain diminish. Even then, he still might say ugly things. Especially if he can't walk again," Dan said thoughtfully.

"His body might heal quickly, but the pain I'm speaking of is in his heart. His heart is broken because the life he loves has been taken from him. His love for flying isn't something he will give up easily or allow to just fade away. He's going to be angry for a very long time and the sooner we all see that, the less hurt we'll find ourselves in the middle of."

Dan shook his head. "You are very wise for such a young woman."

"That and more," Lillie said, hugging Joelle. "You've a very precious love for my son and I've a feeling it will do more to heal his pain than anything else we might do."

*∂*

Later that night, settled into the hotel, Joelle tossed restlessly on her bed. The words she had spoken so confidently in the light of day, seemed trivial and uncertain in the shadows of night.

*What if he never walks? What is he loses his will to live?* The questions raced through Joelle's mind. *What if he stops loving me?*

She pounded the pillow to make it more comfortable, but found little comfort. "Oh, God," she whispered into the stillness of the night, "what am I to do?"

*∂*

John lay in the silence of the hospital room, staring up at the ceiling as he had done for most of the last few days. He had realized that his parents would come, but it had shocked him beyond reason to see Joelle.

He looked down the sheet that covered his legs and tried to force some movement to prove to himself that he was not paralyzed. Nothing moved, however, and his frustration began to mount.

He could imagine Joelle waiting on him day after day, for the rest of their lives. She woul never leave him, he knew that full well. She had too much respectability and compassion. No, she would see him as her mission, John reasoned and he could never let that happen. He did not want her pity and self-suffering. The life he had planned with Joelle had no part in those things.

"I have to make her see reason and leave," John whispered to the ceiling. "Even if I make her hate me, I have to convince her that what we had is over."

Waiting for sleep to come, John wondered how he might accomplish his task. He could be unreasonable and rude. Well, he laughed to himself, he had been that already. It would come quite natural and Joelle would never be ready for it. Little by little, she would see he was no prize and then she would go home. It pained him deeply to imagine the hurt on her face, the sorrow in her heart.

*It's for the best,* he reasoned to himself. *I have to make her stop loving me.*

## four

One week blended quietly into another and the only significant method to mark time was John's steady progress of recovery. Joelle purposefully kept away from the hospital and even after two weeks had passed, she still was not certain how she should handle the situation.

She had spent a great deal of time in thought and prayer. Everything had seemed so simple. Why had God allowed this to happen? Why should John suffer so, when he was so devoted to God's will for his life?

There were few answers for her questions and when Joelle was not sequestered away inside the two-story, concrete "Commercial Hotel," she was reviewing the town. And always, her mind was on John.

"He needs this time," she reasoned to Dan one morning, "to get used to the idea that I'm not going anywhere."

"He asks me every day if you're still here," Dan mused. "I think he's both relieved and unhappy that you haven't come to visit him."

"I'm sure."

Joelle's crisp, white shirtwaist made her face seem strangely pale. Dan wondered silently if she was eating properly. It was already apparent from the dark circles beneath her eyes that sleep was a stranger to her.

"Joelle," Dan said in fatherly overtones, "you have to take care of yourself or you'll be no good at all to John."

"I know," she said with a nod. Going to the hotel window, she stared down at the sandy, isolated town of Columbus.

Settled in the middle of nowhere, four miles north of the Mexican-American border, Columbus, New Mexico was all that Joelle would deem desolate...God-forsaken. It was like one of any number of nondescript towns she had seen while coming south on the train. It was nestled, if that could possibly be the correct word to use, on a vast wasteland of sandy, brown desert. There was nothing to break the monotony but miles of mesquite-dotted flatlands and more cactus than Joelle had ever hoped to see again.

She felt as though she knew every inch of the town by heart, she had paced it out often enough. There was Camp Furlong on the opposite side of the railroad tracks. Resident soldiers in khaki and leather seemed to take an immediate interest in her, even though Joelle gave them no encouragement. She had had no less than five invitations to supper and two less respectable propositions. John would have been livid if he had known.

Joelle had tried not to take offense at their forward manner. Soldiers were soldiers, after all, and some were quite far from home. Also, they were unavoidable and Joelle could not see punishing herself by remaining in the hotel.

While soldiers by far and away made up the largest portion of the town's population, there were other residents, as well. A white-washed bank seemed to do an acceptable amount of business, as well as a handful of shops, several drinking and eating establishments, and, of course, the train depot.

It was quickly revealed that Columbus sported two major events in its daily life—the arrival of The Golden

States Limited, eastbound and its reverse sibling, The Golden States Limited, westbound. The latter was often called the Drunkard Express, due to the fact it brought the furloughed soldiers back from El Paso, some sixty miles to the east. In a town where they enjoyed neither electricity nor telephones, people often turned out in droves to see who or what might arrive by rail.

Joelle, herself, had gone to the yellow train station, given the fact that it possessed the only means of communication with the rest of the world. She had sent two messages by telegram and received two in reply. One came from her brother, Nicholas, and the other from Maggie Lucas. Daughtry was still well and growing larger by the minute and the Lucas family sent their prayers.

"You're at least a million miles away," the voice came from somewhere in her hotel room. Sleepily, Joelle turned from the window and caught her future father-in-law's worried eyes. "And I doubt you've heard a word I've said."

"Sorry," she whispered. "I don't want you to worry about me, Dan. I'm fine. Really, I am. I can't help but think of John and how much he's had to suffer. I know he must be in a great deal of pain and it concerns me that he'll give up and stop trying to get better."

"Let's leave John out of this for a minute. I think you should eat better and get more rest." Dan took a step toward Joelle, then stopped. "We're going to move John to a small house on the edge of town. When we have him settled there, we'll move our things over as well. After that, we'll start preparing him for when those casts come off. You're going to need your strength then. That is, if you plan to help."

"Help? Of course, I'll help, but what can I do?" Joelle voiced the first real interest she had had in the conversation.

"It's going to be difficult to know exactly what will help the most," Dan said. "There are several things we can try. Exercises, hot compresses, salves, and rubs to keep the circulation going, things along those lines. I sent a telegram to a colleague of mine at Walter Reed Hospital in Washington. He's going to collect the latest information in spinal and back injuries and forward it to me."

Just then Lillie returned from the room she shared with Dan. Somehow along the way, Joelle's room had become their gathering place. "Are you ready for supper?" she asked with an expectant glance at Dan and Joelle.

"I believe we are," Dan replied. "I want to discuss John's recovery and supper would provide a good opportunity to do so."

Joelle smiled weakly, knowing Dan's purpose. He intended to see to it that she could not finagle her way out of eating. She quietly followed them downstairs and out into the street.

"I was told by one of the officer's wives," Lillie began, "that they are serving excellent meals at a small cafe just the other side of the newspaper office."

"I'm ready for a change," Dan replied and Joelle nodded. "The hotel serves a substantial fare, but it isn't what I'd call excellent."

They arrived at the quaint establishment and were ushered inside with the greatest of enthusiasm. The robust owner, who introduced himself as Papa Santos, seated them at a small table that held nothing more than a red-and-white checkered cloth and lighted lamp. The soft glow from the table lamps gave the room a cozy feeling and the delectable aroma of spicy Mexican food made even Joelle's mouth water in anticipation.

They ordered from Papa Santos's oral recitation of his menu, then sat back to await their meal. Joelle found that her mind was always on John and, remembering Dan's comments about the move, she questioned him.

"Why are you moving John?" she asked.

"I think the change would be good for him," Dan answered. "He hates the hospital and, frankly, I think they're beginning to hate having him there. I wanted to load him up on the train and move him to El Paso, but the army doctor feels that would be too harsh a trip for him to make. I guess I'm inclined to agree, although I'd like to get all of us out of Columbus."

"Why?" Joelle asked innocently. "Is there some kind of problem here?"

Dan looked at Lillie and the meaningful exchange was not lost on Joelle. She frowned at their silence, biting her lower lip.

Papa Santos seated several new patrons nearby and boisterously acclaimed the restaurant's merits. Dan waited until he had gone before leaning over and continuing. "The area isn't as safe as I'd like it to be," he began. "You know that Mexico is struggling against revolutionaries. They've had all manner of conflict and uprisings and, frankly, it doesn't look good."

Joelle was notably surprised. "Of course, I'd heard about the border raids. I read about them in the paper, but I had no idea we were in any real danger. This is still an

American city. Why should we be afraid here?"

"We're only four miles from the International Boundary at the Palomas Gate and we're the only town of substantial means for miles around. Pancho Villa, the revolutionary responsible for the trouble you read about, is wreaking havoc all along the border and there's no way to tell what he might do next. He's already burned ranches and taken livestock, not to mention—" Dan halted abruptly and coughed. "Well, it probably should be left unmentioned."

Lillie's eyes betrayed her concern. She had already had this conversation with Dan and knew very well what his thoughts were.

"But the army is here to protect us," Joelle rationalized. "Surely this Villa person wouldn't be willing to face down the entire Thirteenth Cavalry."

"They faced worse at Agua Prieta," Dan replied and said nothing more until a plump, dark-skinned woman had settled plates of steaming food in front of each of them. "Shall we ask God's blessing?"

Lillie nodded and bowed her head. Joelle did the same, but not without exchanging another look at Dan's sober expression.

"Father, we thank You for the gifts You have given. We praise You for John's progress and for the bounty that lies before us. We give ourselves over to Your protection and guidance. In Jesus' name, Amen."

"Amen," Lillie whispered.

Joelle's head lifted and her dark eyes bore into Dan's. "What is Agua Prieta?"

"A town just across the border from Douglas, Arizona. Villa was enraged that President Wilson decided to back a man named Carranza as the official leader in Mexico. Villa attacked with ten-thousand men and the *Federales* came from El Paso with equipment our government provided in order to defeat him. They say that after the battle, Villa was down to less than fifteen-hundred men."

"So that's good, isn't it?" Joelle said, picking at the tempting food on her plate.

"It angered Villa even more. He feels the U.S. has betrayed him. At one time they had promised to back him and his people. Villa thought U.S. support would put him in the position of running Mexico. When we withdrew that support, he became just one more revolutionary. Now he has no more prestige in the eyes of our government than do the Red Flaggers."

"Who are they?" Joelle asked.

"Renegades of the worst kind. They're a trashy sort, not at all organized like Villa's men. They carry machetes and flag themselves with red. They are ruthless and even more aggressive than Villa, if that is possible."

"But why do you think they will come here?"

"Camp Furlong has a machine gun unit here. Villa would love to get his hands on those guns. The army knows it, too, and they are looking out for him, but they can't do very much at this point. No one seems to want to authorize any counter action." Dan put down his fork and struggled with an unpleasant thought. "I didn't want to add to the needless worry, so I haven't even told this to Lillie, but just a few days ago, Villa's men attacked a train and hauled off nineteen American mining engineers and killed them. That was at Santa Ysabel, Chihuahua and it isn't that far from Columbus."

"Daniel Monroe!" Lillie said, a look of disbelief crossing her face. "How dare you try to keep things from me. I've been around you long enough to prove myself capable of keeping a cool head. If we're in danger like that, then I should be informed. Maybe moving John is worth the risk."

"Calm down, Lillie." Dan's voice became honey smooth. "You know how I feel about causing you needless pain. I've been leveling with you about most everything. Just hear me out."

Lillie seemed to take a moment to consider his words, then picked up her fork and began to eat. Dan took her lack of comment as acceptance and continued.

"I very much would like to move John out of Columbus, but the situation is such that we could end up permanently damaging his spine. . .maybe even killing him. That's not a risk I'm willing to take and because there is so very little we can tell about his condition, I made the decision to wait things out right here. The army has assured me that they will patrol the area, even on the edges of town, to the utmost. They are increasing their patrols even now."

"Increasing their patrols?" Lillie questioned with a raised brow. "When did you learn about this?"

Dan tried to ignore the tone that told him he would have a great deal to explain when his wife got him alone. "Just a little while ago. So you see, I think the best we can offer John is a homelike atmosphere and an aggressive healing program."

"What can we do for him?" Joelle asked with pleading eyes.

"We can pray and wait with good attitudes and pleasant outlooks. I can't say much more than that. We need to give the broken bones time to heal and also to let John rebuild his strength. After that, we'll have to work the muscles in his legs and hopefully the spinal swelling will go down and we will know the extent of his paralysis."

"I want to help," Joelle stated firmly. "He won't like it and it may seem completely improper, but I want to help. Anyway, it's not like I've never been around grown men. I do have brothers, you know."

Dan glanced at Lillie who wore an I-told-you-so grin on her face. "We knew you'd expect to help," he answered. "So we have decided to take you up on it. See, I have a theory. . .a plan, actually."

Joelle leaned forward. "What kind of plan?"

"You eat everything on your plate," Dan said with a grin, "and I'll tell you."

Joelle's eyes narrowed slightly as her head cocked to one side. "Now I see where John gets it," she said.

"Gets what?"

"His ability to manipulate people into doing what he wants."

Lillie laughed out loud at this and although several people in the room glanced her way, no one seemed at all to mind. Embarrassed by her outburst, nonetheless, Lillie leaned forward and whispered, "John is so much like his father, that at times it's like seeing Dan when he was young."

"You calling me old?"

Lillie glanced from Joelle to Dan. "Never old, Mr. Monroe, just seasoned."

Dan's smile broadened. "That so, Mrs. Monroe," he stated more than questioned. "I guess we might call ourselves a bit spicy, at that."

Joelle had to laugh at their play. She hoped that she and

John would one day find things to laugh about again. An aching in her heart made her want to leave the table and go to his side. But what would he say to her if she showed up in the hospital?

"So," Dan said, momentarily turning from his wife to face Joelle, "you gonna eat?"

Joelle jerked back to the present conversation and nodded. Putting a forkful of food up to her mouth, she spoke. "Start talking, Dr. Monroe."

# five

The small adobe house that Dan secured, was anything but spacious. It had a main living area with a kitchen and front room sharing the same space and two small bedrooms off the back. There was, of course, no indoor plumbing, but then Joelle had not seen the likes of that since living with her parents in Kansas City.

Joelle could not help but think of her mother and father as she watched Dan and Lillie work to ready the house for John. They had not wanted to let her come to New Mexico to live with Nick and Daughtry. It was only after a series of letters from Nicholas and the united efforts of Joelle and her older sister, Natalie, that Riley and Zandy Dawson had agreed to let their youngest leave home. They understood her need to be on her own and this choice had kept her from sprouting wings and flying too far from their watchful eye. And, while Nick and Daughtry received a live-in nanny and housemaid, Joelle got to be nearer to John.

Seeing Dan stop to steal a quiet kiss from his wife, Joelle made a mental note to send her parents a telegram when time permitted. They would want to know about John's condition, Joelle reasoned, and it might help ease her home-sickness for them.

The move from the hospital to the house came in February and Joelle was on hand to see to it that John got properly tucked into the small but firm bed that Dan had personally made for him. Dan and Lillie had already agreed that Joelle should have the first chance at some private time with John once he was settled in. They started to leave the room, but John called out and stopped them.

"I thought I asked you to send Joelle home," John said with a glaring frown.

Joelle smiled warmly. "I told you I was staying put until you could make me leave. From the looks of you that ought to be a good long while."

John grimaced and muttered something inaudible under his breath. "You gonna let her torment me like this?" he asked, turning to his father and mother.

"I think she's earned the right to stay," Dan said. "In fact, I think it might do you two some good to have a few moments alone. Come on, Lillie."

"I don't want a few moments alone!" John yelled after his parents' retreating forms. "Do you hear me? Take her with you!"

Joelle closed the door behind Lillie and Dan, thinking as she did that she heard Dan laugh. Turning slowly and smoothing her muslin apron, she faced John.

"I gave you plenty of time to get used to my being here. You can't force me to leave you, John. You might as well stop fussing about it and accept the fact that I'm here and here I'm going to stay." Joelle kept her expression rigid and firm.

"I don't want you here!" His words were harsh and painful to Joelle's ears, but she swallowed her hurt and squared her shoulders. John knew, by the look in her eyes, that his words had hit their mark. He refused to back down, however. He had to convince her to leave.

"I'm staying, anyway," Joelle said with renewed determination.

"I told you to leave," he countered. The firm set of his jaw told Joelle he meant business, but there was something very boyish in his expression and this made Joelle smile. "You think I'm joking about this?" John asked, growing angrier by the minute.

"I think you're a little boy with his nose out of joint," Joelle replied. "Why don't you stop feeling sorry for yourself, John Monroe, and put that effort into getting better?"

"You don't seem to understand. I might not get better!" he proclaimed in a voice nearly loud enough to rattle the windowpanes.

"You don't understand," Joelle declared, coming to stand directly over him. "I. . .don't. . .care!" And with those words the shouting match was on.

"You're leaving!"

"I'm staying!"

"I mean it, Joelle!"

"So do I, John!"

"I'll make you miserable until you get back on that train and go home!"

"No doubt!" Joelle's tiny voice was no match for John's but she put her heart and soul into the matter and found herself quite capable of holding her own. "Just go ahead and try!"

"If I could get out of this bed, I'd be tempted to throttle you!"

"If you could move out of that bed, we wouldn't be having this conversation!"

"Joelle, you're making me angry and you aren't getting

anywhere with this. I'm going to tell Dad to get you packed and on the next available train. Now, for the last time, I want you to go."

"For the last time?" Joelle questioned. "What a relief. I thought you might keep up this foolery for weeks to come." She leaned her face down, coming within inches of his face. Her voice softened and a loving smile touched her face. "You can tell me to go, but you can't make me leave. I love you, John, and your angry words and self-pity aren't going to change it one bit."

Without warning, Joelle pressed her lips against John's. She felt him resist, keeping himself aloof and refusing to return her kiss, but it did not cause her a moment's hesitation. Gently, she continued to kiss him until she felt his hands on her arms and the hardness of his mouth soften. Feeling him surrender his anger, Joelle broke away and stared at him for a moment.

"I'm staying," she whispered and pulled herself away from John's touch.

John closed his eyes, refusing to look at her. "Don't do it, Joelle. I'm only thinking of you. It's gonna be a long, hard haul, don't think I don't know it."

Joelle sighed. "I never thought it would be easy, but my love for you will get me through."

John's fury was back and his voice was a growl. "Your love will turn to pity. In fact, it probably already has. You just feel sorry for me. Isn't that true?" His accusation infuriated Joelle.

"Ha!" Joelle exclaimed and John's eyes snapped open. Seeing she had his full attention, Joelle nearly danced to the door. "The last thing in the world I feel for you is pity.

You may have every other woman swooning over you with sad-faced sympathy, but not me. I know what you're capable of and I won't be charmed into letting you get out of it. When you're out of that cast, I'll expect a great deal of work out of you, John Monroe, and pity won't take you very far."

John was obviously surprised at her outburst, but he steadied his voice. "Go home, Joelle, and leave me alone."

"No," Joelle replied simply and waltzed out the door, closing it behind her.

"Joelle!" John yelled from the other side. Joelle leaned against the whitewashed adobe wall and sighed. She was not aware of Dan and Lillie watching her, until Lillie spoke.

"He's not going to make this easy on you, is he?"

Joelle shoved her hands deep into her apron pockets. "He thinks he has the upper hand, but I can already tell that you were right. If we can just channel his anger into determination to get out of that bed, he'll be on his feet in no time at all."

"It could get ugly," Dan reminded her.

Joelle sobered. "It could never be as ugly as him lying there, rotting away and feeling sorry for himself. I can endure his temper and his insults. He doesn't mean a single word of it, anyway. I'll stick it out and when it's all over and he's back on his feet, John will owe me the nicest honeymoon trip to San Francisco that an army pilot's money can buy."

Lillie laughed. "Spoken like a true woman!"

Dan rolled his eyes. "That's for sure."

❧

Within a matter of days, the four of them fell into a companionable routine. For Joelle, mornings were spent fixing breakfast while Dan and Lillie examined and bathed John. Each day, Dan charted John's progress and reported it to the army doctor, who in turn reported it back to John's superiors at Fort Bliss.

Dan devised a series of exercises for John that were designed to strengthen his arms. He reasoned with his son that once the swelling around the spine had sufficiently decreased, the time would come when John would need the extra muscle.

John was not the best patient and Joelle often told him so. She refused to give him a single bit of sympathy and John's frustration with her presence seemed to take on new life.

"Did you enjoy your breakfast?" Joelle asked, coming into John's room.

"Did you make it?"

"Why yes, I did," Joelle replied sweetly.

"I figured as much," John said, looking away. The fact was, he had enjoyed the breakfast very much, but he was not about to let her know that. He had to force himself at times just to keep up the façade of being angry with her, in hopes that she would go home. Now was no exception, especially in light of the way she looked.

"Look at the mess you made," Joelle chided, coming to retrieve his breakfast tray. "I suppose next thing you know, I'll have to feed you as well as fix your meals."

"Nobody asked you to fix anything. In fact, nobody even asked you to be here," John stated in a low voice. His anger was evident, yet he still tried to tidy the messiness around his tray while stealing glances at Joelle.

She swept his hands away and took the task in hand,

trying again to get some response regarding his food. "Did you enjoy your omelette? I got the recipe from a bona fide French chef." John said nothing, but seeing that he had eaten every bit of it, Joelle smiled. "I guess you did."

He watched her cross the room and thought that there had never been a more beautiful woman alive. He allowed himself to linger on her turned back, wishing he could touch the long, dark braid that bound her hair. *I can't do this to her,* he thought angrily. *I have to get her away from me.* With a heavy sigh he faced Joelle as she turned back to the bed. "Joelle, when are you going to get tired of playing nursemaid?"

"When are you going to get tired of playing invalid?" she shot back at him without so much as a blink of her eyes.

A noticeable tick in John's cheek warned Joelle that his wrath was not far behind. "I'm not playing at anything," he growled.

"Neither am I," she mimicked his tones.

"Joelle!"

"John!" she countered and paused to rid the bed of the remaining toast crumbs. Reaching out to brush the bits away, she found her wrist encircled with John's steel-like grip.

"I see you're gaining hand strength," she said, refusing to flinch under the increasing pressure. "Those exercises must be paying off."

"Go home, Joelle."

"I am home, John. Wherever you are, that's my home." Her words were soft and sure and it was John who flinched and lost his nerve. Joelle's eyes were dark and her face was flushed from their confrontation.

"Don't look at me like that," he moaned, releasing her arm.

"Like what?" Joelle asked, straightening up.

"Never mind, just get out of here."

"I was going, but I'll be back after I wash the dishes. I'm going to help you with some new exercises," she said and went to retrieve the tray.

"Oh no, you're not," John declared. "Mom or Dad can do that."

"Your father has been asked by the army doctor to give him a hand at the hospital. Your mother is out shopping for some of the things we need. So you see, there is no one else and the exercises must be done." She stared back at him so matter-of-factly that John could think of no reply.

"Now, finish your coffee and I'll be back shortly." She handed him his cup and turned to retrieve the tray.

"It's not going to work, Joelle."

Joelle paused at the door. "What's not going to work, beloved?" she asked innocently.

"This game you and my folks are playing. You think you can make me well by the sheer will of your desires and it's not going to work. I may never walk again. You have to face facts."

"I do believe you're afraid to walk again. What's the matter, John? Can't bear the thought of having to face your army buddies and explain the crash?" John's jaw dropped and Joelle immediately wanted to take the words back. She did not like being contrary, especially when all she wanted to do was take him in her arms and hold him close. She wanted to convince him that if he stayed in a bed the rest of his life, she would still love him, but Dan had assured her there was nothing productive in that.

Steadying herself to keep the confrontational spirit alive, Joelle appeared almost smug at his continued silence. "I thought so. I've faced the fact that you might never walk again, John darling. But I think you haven't been able to face the fact that you very well may." With that she left the room, pulling the door closed. She had barely taken a step toward the kitchen when the reverberating crash of John's coffee mug hit the door behind her.

Setting the tray on the table, Joelle went back to John's room and opened the door enough to survey the shattered pieces of the cup. "Well, at least you drank the coffee. It makes less of a mess to clean up." Seeing John clench his fist, Joelle only smiled. "I'll tell your mom we'd better lay in a supply of cups."

Before approaching John's room again, Joelle finished the dishes and tidied the rest of the room. She was weary of their fighting, but she knew that a spark of life had come back into John, which Dr. Dan had said had been absent after the crash.

In the hospital, Dan had told her, John had become quite complacent with his injuries. He was angry, yes, but totally uncooperative when it came to working through the healing process. He wanted no one to touch him and he refused to allow the doctor to so much as to suggest the future possibilities of using a wheelchair or crutches. Now, Joelle knew full well that the exercises Dan had devised for John were intentionally designed to progress him toward one or the other of those very subjects. God help them all, when John figured it out.

"Are you ready to get to work?" Joelle asked, coming

into the room.

"I told you I wasn't going to work with you and I won't."

"The sooner you cooperate, the sooner I'll leave you alone."

"For good?" John asked her blatantly.

For the first time, John's words had cut her to the quick. Joelle was speechless for a moment. Was that the price of John's recovery? Did she dare to push him so hard that his resentment of her interference would forever sever their relationship? Was she killing their love?

Joelle studied him for a moment. The swelling had gone from his face and the healthy color had returned. For all intent and purpose, he looked the picture of health, except for the fact that he was in a cast and still unable to feel anything below the waist.

With tears in her eyes, Joelle made her decision. "If that's the price to see you walking again, then so be it." She turned away from him to retrieve some hand weights that Dan had fashioned and she dabbed the tears from her eyes.

"I'm sorry, Joelle."

The words caught her off guard and her tears started anew. It was the first civil thing he had said to her since the accident. Refusing to acknowledge them, she froze.

"I didn't mean to hurt you. This isn't fair to either one of us, but then I suppose nothing in life guarantees us fairness." He paused for a moment. "I can't bear to think of you married to me like this. You're young and alive and healthy and whole and you deserve to be with someone who is likewise. I can't give you the future you deserve. Can't you try to understand that?"

Joelle swallowed hard and turned to face him. The tears

on her cheeks glistened when the sunlight from the window fell across her face. Her voice was but a whisper as she spoke. "Rise up, my love, my fair one, and come away. For, lo, the winter is past, the rain is over and gone."

Their eyes met. "Joelle," he groaned in a sad, childlike way, "please don't do this to me."

What all of John's anger could not accomplish, these simple words did. Broken completely, Joelle dropped the weights to the floor and fled the room with a sob.

## six

It was in the middle of the night when John woke the house with his anguished cries of pain. Lillie and Joelle both came running from the room they shared to find Dan bent over his son, rapidly massaging his right thigh.

"What is it!" Lillie exclaimed.

Both women were surprised when Dan turned to face them with a grin. "He's got a cramp in his leg and he feels it!"

Lillie and Joelle exchanged looks of astonishment. "He feels it!" Lillie said to Joelle. "Isn't that wonderful?"

"It doesn't feel so wonderful from this end of it, Mom."

Lillie moved to her son's bedside. "I hope it hurts enough to give you the desire to regain what you once had. I don't want you to live in pain, but I want you to feel everything that happens to that leg, for the rest of your life."

John looked up to meet his mother's eyes. "Me, too, Mom." He winced painfully. "Me, too."

Joelle stood back by the door and watched the scene. John caught sight of her in the amber glow of the room. She was wearing a long white gown with a soft blue shawl drawn around her. Her long dark hair, usually pinned neatly in a bun, fell in a swirl of curls to her hips and John longed to touch the chestnut softness. She was the most beautiful sight he had ever beheld and in that moment, he was glad that she had refused to leave him.

When their eyes met, it was like he was seeing her for the

first time and after the words they had exchanged earlier in the day, he could tell Joelle was still feeling cautious.

The cramp passed and everyone made their way back to bed. It was a long time before Joelle could drift back to sleep, however. She had seen the look in John's eyes and knew that he still loved her. The thing that troubled her most, however, was wondering if she was truly doing the right thing in staying. Maybe she was more torture to him, than help. How could she possible know?

Within her heart, a voice seemed to whisper, *Trust Me, Joelle*. She knew instantly that the voice was not of her own doing. A peace began to filter through her body and within minutes she was fast asleep.

ক

The following morning brought a fierce wind that blew the sand about in such a vicious way that it nearly stripped the whitewash from the bank. It was nothing compared to the true sand storms of the spring, folks assured Lillie and Joelle, but nevertheless, it was torturous and required that all of the windows be closed tight against the assault.

It was in the midst of this onslaught when a visitor arrived at the Monroe house. The weather-worn man quickly introduced himself as John's superior from Fort Bliss.

"Major Camstead, ma'am," the man said upon entry. He removed his peaked campaign hat and tucked it under his arm. "I arrived this morning on business at Camp Furlong and they told me I might find Lieutenant Monroe here."

Lillie smiled at the man. "Yes, my son is here. He's still recovering from his accident, but I'm sure they told you this."

"Yes, ma'am," he replied. "I would like to speak with

him about the accident, if you think he's up to it."

Joelle moved to the bedroom door. "I'll check and see if he's awake."

Lillie nodded, while Joelle went in to announce the major's arrival to John. "I'm certain my son will be happy for the company, Major. Lately, he's seen little of anyone but family."

"Speaking of family," the major mumbled, reaching into his pocket, "Sergeant Monroe sends his regards." He handed an envelope to Lillie.

"It's from J.D.?" she questioned, then noted the handwriting. "How kind of you to bring it all this way. Thank you, Major."

The man blushed and feeling quite uncertain as to what he should do next, was greatly relieved when Joelle returned. "He's awake and said to join him at your convenience."

Major Camstead dismissed himself with a curt nod. "Ma'am," he said to Lillie and then again to Joelle as he passed to the bedroom. At the door he paused long enough to close it, much to the disappointment of both Lillie and Joelle.

Giving John a brief once over, Camstead grinned. "Well, Preacher, looks like you made a mess of yourself this time," he said, coming to pull a chair along John's bed.

"You're a long way from home, Bob," John replied, using his hands to push himself up on the pillows. The informality he took with the major had long ago been agreed upon between them.

"Had business with the Thirteenth and thought a visit to you was in order. How's it coming?"

"Slow," John replied. "Way too slow."

"Give it time. You can't expect everything your way. Say, that little brown-eyed beauty out there," Camstead said with a nod, "she doesn't belong to you, does she?"

John's grin broadened to a full-blown smile. "As a matter of fact, she does."

"Some guys have all the luck."

John nodded uncomfortably. "But you didn't come all this way to talk about my love life, now did you?"

"No, actually I wanted to know about the crash. Wanna tell me about it willing or shall I order you around?" He smiled and John shook his head.

"I'm not sure I could take an order seriously. I can salute, but I sure can't get up and snap to."

"I'll take the story," the man replied. "You can salute me later."

John laughed, but thoughts of the accident sobered him rather quickly. "I was at about fifteen-hundred feet when she started handling rough. The whole engine seemed like it was going to shake right out from the cowling. I shut her down to see what I could make of it and when the prop was slowed to where it was just windmilling, I could see it had splintered apart. There was a good six inches missing off the end on one side."

"We're having a bad time of that down here. The air's so dry it's causing us to have to remove the props and put them in humidified rooms to keep them from coming unglued."

"Well, I wish you'd have figured that out before it happened to me."

"Me, too, John. You don't know how sorry I was to hear about your crash."

John met his friend's eyes. They had known each other

for little over a year now, but Major Robert Camstead had quickly become one of John's closest comrades-in-arms.

"I'm glad you came, Bob," John said, trying to move the conversation away from the maudlin. "I sure didn't know how I'd get to you."

"Is there anything you need that you aren't getting around here?"

"No, I have it all. Two beautiful women waiting on me hand and foot. My own, personal physician and plenty of creature comforts. Who could ask for more?" John replied.

"Well, I promised J.D. I'd check you out in person," Bob said, referring to John's brother. "In fact, I just handed over a letter from him to your mother."

"Will you be here a while?"

"No. Duty calls and I have to get back in time to catch the eastbound."

"You mean to tell me you didn't fly over?" John questioned in disbelief.

"In case you haven't noticed, there's a sand storm blowing around out there. It isn't a bad one, but I sure wouldn't attempt to fly through the thing. Besides, I came by train last night and that's the way they expect me to make it back."

"Yeah, well take the sand with you all the way back to Fort Bliss."

"For you, my boy, anything," Bob said and extended his hand. "John, you let us know if you need something. Anything at all, okay?"

"Sure. You know me. I never hesitate to speak my mind."

Bob paused, John's hand still firmly planted against his own. "It's a good thing God was watching over you when Jenny decided to dump you."

A frown crossed John's face. "He may have been watching, but to my way of thinking, He almost missed catching me."

"Those are strange words coming from you, Preacher."

"No stranger than the circumstance that gave them thought," John countered. "Tell J.D. I'm doing well and don't forget to ask my mother if she has any messages for him."

"I'll do that, John." Major Camstead released his hand, gave a brief salute, and left the room.

It was only moments before Joelle appeared. "You look tired, John. Why don't you try to get some rest?"

John glanced up at her for a moment. Things had changed between them since he had made her cry. He was more careful how he responded now. "I am tired, but no more so than you, I imagine. You don't look like you're getting much sleep."

Joelle defensively raised her hand to her face. "This is a harsh country, John. It isn't at all what I'm used to. The heat is starting to build and the dryness is hard on my complexion." Her words sounded formal and stiff.

"You're still the best looking woman I've ever laid eyes on," John replied, surprising them both. To cover up his embarrassment, he added, "Now get out of here and let me sleep."

Joelle did just that, smiling as she closed his door quietly behind her. He was more and more like the John she had fallen in love with. Soon, she thought to herself, soon she would have him back and he would walk again.

❧

March, 1916 roared in like a lion and continued to roar. The temperature rose, becoming quite uncomfortable in the afternoon. Used to the chillier mountain valley winters of Bandelero, Lillie and Joelle found their clothing heavy and cumbersome. Deeming that the heat would be much easier to bear in appropriate clothing, the women took Dan's suggestion and went shopping.

"Get something serviceable," Lillie suggested. "Something easy to wash out by hand and light enough to dry quickly."

"In this dry heat," Joelle said, mopping her damp brow, "everything dries quickly."

Lillie smiled. "It certainly isn't home. I miss the snow and our cold mornings. Dan calls it 'cuddle weather' and I think it's about my favorite time of year."

"You and Dr. Dan sure seem happy with each other," Joelle said with a sigh. "I just wish John could see that I love him and accept the fact that I want to be with him no matter what his physical condition is."

Lillie paused in her consideration of a ready-made skirt. "John knows you love him, Joelle. It's just hard for him to think of disappointing you. His love for you runs deep and he takes everything very seriously. Marriage is no exception."

"I know," Joelle said and there were tears in her eyes. "It's just that I'm afraid he's going to put up a permanent barrier between us. I'm afraid. . . ," her voice cracked and Lillie put an arm around her.

"Don't be. God will help John to make it through this. Have patience and faith." Joelle wiped at her eyes and nodded. Lillie smiled. "Now, what do you think about this green skirt?"

Rumors of the war in Europe flooded the pages of the local newspaper and even in the local theater propaganda ran rampant. *The Beasts in Gray* was advertised for viewing at two bits a person, no children allowed. Women were discouraged from attending the picture with the ghastly posters outside the theater depicting the Huns in spiked helmets, tearing at the puritanical white robes of Belgian women. Joelle shuddered at the thought of what those poor European women must be enduring, but she said nothing to anyone about it. Somehow, with it left unsaid, it seemed less real and more easily to deal with.

The saggy iron bed, with its groaning springs and lumpy mattress, became less and less appealing to Joelle, as night after night passed. Lillie, too, grew tired of the poor substitute. At home, she had a fine, down-filled mattress that was as soft and comfortable as any bed had ever been. This, combined with the growing heat, was beginning to wear thin on her nerves and caused Daniel to begin seeking a way, once again, to move John from Columbus.

By the eighth of March, the Monroes and Joelle had shared their cramped quarters for nearly one month. John had made remarkable improvements. He now had feeling in his legs and although he was unable to walk, he endured hours of exercises devised by his father.

John and Joelle still had their occasional fight, but John admittedly came to realize just how much she had done for him. It was still hard for him to accept the fact that she had seen him at his worst, but even this humiliation was passing from John's concern. Now, uppermost in his mind, was to strengthen the tender threads that bound his heart to hers.

"I have tickets for us to leave on the twentieth," Dan shared that night after supper. "I even managed to secure a private car, thanks to Garrett Lucas."

Lillie smiled. "Had one sitting in the backyard, did he?"

Dan laughed. "Just about. You know how Garrett is. He's always managed to get his hands on just about whatever he needs. Anyway, he's making the arrangements to have the car put on and brought down for the trip home. This way, I can keep John in bed for most of the trip. I think he'll manage quite well with it."

"Well I for one, will not miss this heat and sand," Joelle said. "May I go tell John the news?"

"Sure," Dan said, sharing a smile with his wife. "Go on and tell him."

Joelle knocked lightly at the open door to John's room. No doubt he had already heard the exchange, but Joelle decided they needed to discuss the future.

"Hello," Joelle said, trying her best to gauge what kind of mood John was in.

"Hello." His voice was warm, almost mellow and Joelle felt her heart skip a beat as John's eyes appraised her appearance.

"Did you hear your father's news? We're going home on the twentieth."

"Yes," John said softly, "I heard."

"I thought it might be good for us to discuss what happens when we return to Bandelero."

"What do you mean?" John questioned.

"Well," Joelle said slowly, "I thought it might be good for us to go ahead and get married." She held her breath for a moment, wondering if John would launch into a tirade.

When he remained silent, she continued. "I mean, it just makes sense. I plan to be a part of your recovery. I certainly don't intend to go back to the ranch with my brother and Daughtry. I don't want to ever be that far away from you again." She felt as though she was rambling, but the fear of letting John speak something negative kept her talking.

"I'd be happy to live with your folks for however long it takes to get you up on your feet."

Here, John interrupted. "That might never happen. I told you once before, Joelle, I may never walk again."

Joelle nodded. "I know, but it doesn't matter to me. I still love you, John, in spite of everything we've gone through of late. I don't mind the fights we've had or the harsh words, but I don't want to be cast aside like old, worn-out boots."

John laughed out loud at this. "You're the best looking worn boots I've ever seen." Joelle blushed but cast John a shy smile. John sobered at the look. "You really are beautiful. Too beautiful to spend your life being a nursemaid to an invalid. I can't make you honor a promise you made when there was so much more hope to our future."

Joelle shook her head. "I have no future without you. Don't you understand? You're everything to me. Whether you walk or talk or run in circles. It doesn't matter."

"I can't expect you to understand, Joelle. You're a woman."

"And just what is that suppose to mean?"

"If I can't walk, I can't very well put bread on the table, now can I?" His voice held a bit of sarcasm and Joelle felt angry that he had taken such a tone with her.

"What's wrong with me getting a job? I could take in sewing or maybe open a shop. There are all kinds of possibilities. I know my father would advance me the money to start a business, if I asked him to."

John shook his head furiously. "No! I won't support a wife on the charity of others. My folks caring for me is bad enough. I certainly won't ask them to support a wife, as well."

"I didn't ask you to," Joelle snapped. "I've already told you that I'd be happy to support us. I just want there to be an 'us,' don't you understand?" she questioned, emphasizing the word "you."

"It wouldn't be right, Joelle. You and I both know what's expected of a husband and having you out doing my job wouldn't be right. Think of what people would say and how it would look."

"Since when have you ever cared what people had to say?"

"I care, Joelle. I care because I know it would hurt you. Besides, you've talked a million times of wanting to have a family. A large family, as I recall. You can't have that with me. At least not now, maybe never." John shook his head again. "I honestly believe it's best if you go home to your brother and then go on back to Kansas City. If I do recover and you're still available, then perhaps—"

"Perhaps nothing, John Monroe!" Joelle crossed the room to the door. "I don't want to hear any more of this. I refuse your solutions." She stormed out of the room and slammed the door behind her.

"Joelle!" John called. "Joelle be reasonable!"

Dan and Lillie exchanged a look as Joelle continued to

the room she shared with Lillie, where she again slammed
the door behind her.

&

That evening, as Joelle prepared for bed, she found herself
thinking of John and what he had said. She did not want to
admit that his words had any basis in truth, but in the quiet
of her room, the evidence of that seemed blatantly obvious.

How much longer would it be before he could walk? His
spine seemed to have fared better than anyone could possibly have hoped and even Dan seemed confident that John's
recovery was just a matter of time. But what if it wasn't?
What if it was as John had said. . .that something might never
happen?

Doffing her cotton day dress, Joelle slipped into her nightgown and slowly braided her hair. The heat, which was so
unbearable during the day, was quickly replaced with the
chill of the desert. Once the sun was down, Joelle was quite
happy to light a fire in the stove and hover around it while
fixing supper. A soldier friend of John's had even told her
that the water often froze in their canteens overnight, but
Joelle found it hard to imagine when the heat of day bore
down on the small village.

Outside her still-open window, Joelle could hear the *clip-
clop* of several horses and knew it was the cavalry patrol
riding their nightly vigil. It made her feel safe to know they
were so carefully watched over and even though the house
was situated on the edge of the town, the army clearly honored their duty to protect all of the citizens of Columbus.

Extinguishing her lamp, Joelle crawled into bed and
drifted off to sleep. She was not aware when Lillie came
to bed, but she did wake up when the army doctor sent an

orderly to request Dan's help in surgery. Lillie got Dan's bag, while he finished dressing, and Joelle fell back to sleep without even hearing Dan leave.

In her dreams, Joelle heard the rush of water as though a flood were bearing down on their tiny hut. The sound rapidly changed to that of horses' hooves and, suppressing a scream, Joelle bolted upright in bed.

The thunderous noise had been no dream. Lillie shot out of the bed with a cry and Joelle quickly followed her to the door. Without opening it, they huddled against it, listening for several moments.

"What's happening? Is it the army?" Joelle questioned breathlessly. She reached out to pull the curtain back from the window when shots rang out. "Is it Villa's men?" Joelle asked, cowering in fear.

At the sound of gunfire, Lillie grabbed Joelle's hand. "It doesn't sound like they're friendly, whoever they are."

Just then, John's voice rang out. "Mom! Joelle! Where are you?"

Lillie pulled Joelle with her to John's room. By now, the predawn silence was filled with gunfire and Spanish curses. Lillie shuddered when a voice rang out just outside their window.

"Death to gringo soldiers!" the voice yelled. It was soon joined by another. "Kill them all!"

Joelle turned to Lillie. "We have to hide John," she said urgently.

"I'm not going anywhere," John answered, coming to the edge of his bed.

"John, you can't fight anyone in your condition. Those men are seeking the blood of soldiers and you are a soldier.

Joelle is right," Lillie said firmly. "We have to hide you."

"Just give me a gun," John protested.

"We don't have a gun," Joelle replied. "The closet, Lillie, we can get him into the closet."

Lillie nodded. "I'll get his right arm, you get his left. John, you keep your feet under you and help us as much as you can."

John shook his head, but found his mother very determined. "I'm not a coward. I can't let you face them alone. If they were to come in here—"

Gunshots sounded loudly and Joelle cringed. The army Hotchkiss machine guns fired off a rapid reply, but it did little to ease the worry of either woman.

Joelle and Lillie were already moving John toward the closet when the sound of someone trying to push in the front door caught their attention. There was another shout of curses and orders in Spanish that only John understood in full.

"They're going to knock the door in," he said flatly.

"Hurry, Lillie," Joelle whispered and nearly pulled John's arm out of its socket. "You get in there with John and I'll go hold them off."

"Don't do this," John said, looking down at Joelle. "Stay here with me. You can't fight them, Joelle. You don't know what these animals are capable of."

"They're capable of killing you," Joelle said quite frankly. "Anything else, anything at all, is preferable to that."

She shoved John into the closet, feeling a twinge of guilt when he lost his balance and slipped to the floor. Lillie stepped over his legs and crouched down beside him.

"It's a tight fit, but it'll work," she whispered to Joelle.

"Good. Don't come out, no matter what you hear. You have to keep John here, Lillie. Please don't let him act heroic." Joelle's eyes pleaded with Lillie. Each woman understood the anguish of the other. Both were fighting to save the life of the man they loved more dearly than life itself.

"No, don't let her go out there," John was struggling against his mother and trying to ease past her in the darkness.

Joelle closed the closet door, sealing them inside. Silently, she prayed it would not become their tomb.

## seven

"You have to stop her," John said, taking hold of his mother's shoulders. He could not see anything in the blackness of their hiding place, but he knew she was facing him.

"John, there's nothing we can do. If you expose yourself, they'll kill you. For Joelle's sake, if not mine, please be quiet. Maybe they'll leave when they see no one else is here."

The noise outside grew louder as shouts of American soldiers rallied hope in the night.

"Dear God, what have I done?" John moaned and slumped back against the closet wall. "If only I would have—"

"Hush, John," Lillie insisted with her hand to his lips. "'If onlys' are behind us. We can't change what is. This is the time to give up the past. This is the time to maybe go to God about those things you said."

John realized how right she was. "I was so angry when the plane started to fall from the sky. I couldn't control her well enough. I should have been able to. I blamed God for letting me crash. I said—"

"John, it doesn't matter. Take it back to Him and seek His forgiveness," Lillie said softly. She put her arm around his shoulders and pulled him close. "He already knows how sorry you are. Let it go, John. Let Him forgive you."

John knew she was right. It was all he had wanted from

the start. Why had he allowed his anger to eat away at him? Why had he allowed his self-pity and frustration to separate him from Joelle? There was so much he wanted to say to her, so much he needed to tell her. Only now, there might not ever be a chance to do so.

They could hear the pounding and gunfire outside the house. John sought God in prayer and Lillie did the same. They heard the front door give way, followed by the yipping and howls of several men. Joelle was protesting loudly that she was alone and that the soldiers were already on their way to protect her.

John gripped Lillie's hand hard, completely unaware of the pain he caused her. Lillie was almost grateful for the pain for John's clutch kept her from jumping to her feet and running to Joelle's side. How could she allow her to face those men alone?

The voices grew louder, with Joelle's shouted protests.

"I should go to her," Lillie whispered.

"No," John said. "It's bad enough she's out there, but if you join her, they'll probably kill you both. I can't bear it as it is. Please, Mom, stay here with me."

Lillie put her free hand over his. She opened her mouth to reply when Joelle's screams filled the house. John struggled to move to the door, but Lillie held him back, using her body as a block between him and his goal.

"No! No!" Lillie said as loudly as she dare. "John, stay here."

Joelle screamed again and several gunshots rang out. There were shouts and the sound of glass breaking and then after a while the noise grew strangely silent. Lillie wondered if Joelle had run from the house to escape her attackers, while John prayed as he had never before prayed, for the safety of the only woman he would ever love.

Time passed in the pounding beats of their own hearts. Lillie had no idea how long they had been in the closet. She had no way of knowing if the sun had yet come up or if it was still dark outside. It felt like the world had come to a standstill and a nightmarish eternity had somehow begun.

The gunfire continued, though much more sporadically than before and the undeniable smell of smoke was heavy on the air.

"I'd better see what's going on," Lillie told John. "If they've set enough fires, we might be in danger of burning up."

"Let me."

Lillie pushed John back again. "You can't. You may have already injured yourself. Please, John, just stay here. I'll be right back."

Lillie opened the closet door the barest crack and found a faint glow of light giving view to the bedroom. No one seemed to be there and so Lillie eased the door open and crawled out.

Her muscles ached from the cramped quarters and awkward positioning. She was not a young girl anymore and it grieved her to feel the reminder. Favoring her right leg, which had fallen asleep beneath her, Lillie tried to tiptoe to the bedroom door.

Putting her ear to the wood, Lillie listened and heard nothing. *Do I open it or not?* she wondered silently. A sound behind her caused Lillie to start and step back. John appeared in the doorway of the closet.

"Listen!" he said in a voice just above a whisper. "They're leaving."

"How do you know?" Lillie questioned. She could speak very little Spanish even after all her years in New Mexico.

John crawled out into the room. "They're retreating. The army must have them on the run."

Lillie moved quickly to the window. "I can't tell what's happening," she moaned. "It's still too dark to tell. The sun's coming up, but I just can't make it all out."

"They're leaving, I'm sure of it. Find Joelle, Mom. Find her and make sure she's all right," John said, pulling himself to the side of his bed.

Lillie nodded. "John, you should stay in the closet until we're sure about what's happening."

"I'm all right," he said and motioned to the closed bedroom door. "Just find Joelle."

Lillie moved cautiously and turned the knob of the door as silently as she could. Peering out into the front room, Lillie could not make out a single thing except the faint glow of dawn against the front door opening.

"Joelle?" she whispered the name. A rush of mounted men raced past the front door, causing Lillie to momentarily pull back. Once they were gone, however, she pressed forward into the room.

Picking her way through the debris of overturned chairs and table, Lillie called again. "Joelle, are you here?"

Nothing. The silence was maddening and Lillie knew she dared not light a lamp. Getting on her hands and knees, Lillie moved through the mess into the shadowy corners of the room. Her heart nearly stopped when her hand felt the warm touch of flesh.

"Joelle!" she exclaimed, but there was no reply.

Lillie ran her hand across the unmistakable feminine form.

"Joelle, speak to me. Joelle," Lillie reached down and pulled the unconscious form to her breast. She felt revulsion as Joelle's nightgown fell away from her body in a tattered heap.

"Oh, God, no," Lillie moaned, rocking Joelle back and forth. "Oh, please, God, help us."

No longer caring whether anyone saw the light, Lillie raced to her untouched bedroom and got the lamp and one of her own nightgowns.

"Mother!" John yelled, sensing that all was not well. "What's going on out there?"

"Hush, John. Please be still, Joelle's hurt." Lillie knew that with her son's determination she might very well see him crawling through the doorway at any moment. Lighting the lamp and putting it to one side, Lillie dressed Joelle's battered body in the nightdress and eased her back to the floor.

Lillie assessed the situation gravely. Joelle had been hit repeatedly across the face. There were multiple bruises already forming and her lips were bloody. She was mercifully unconscious and Lillie could only pray that she had been that way throughout her attack.

"John, I have to find your father," Lillie said, coming to her son. "I'm going to get you into bed and go after him."

"Don't bother with me," John said sternly. "What about Joelle?"

"She's hurt."

"Is it bad?"

"Yes," Lillie replied gravely. "I'm afraid it's very bad, John."

"This is all my fault!" he yelled and pounded the bedframe

with his fist. "All my fault!"

"John, it doesn't matter who you blame. It certainly won't change matters now. Joelle needs help and I have to find your father. This isn't any more your fault than it is mine. The madmen who shot up the town are the ones we can blame for this fiasco. Now, stay here," Lillie instructed.

His mother's words rang over and over in his head. John was spent from crawling to the bed from the closet, but now he prayed for the strength to go to Joelle.

"I have to be there for her, Lord," he whispered. Making a slow, but steady progress to the door, John was consumed with guilt. He had brought her here. His accident had caused her to rush to his side.

"I told her to go home," he muttered, moving inch by painful inch. "I begged her to leave this place."

John concentrated on each movement. Pull with the right arm. Pull with the left. His legs, still weak and mostly useless to his efforts, dragged behind him like a seal crossing a beach.

He was through the bedroom door when he saw her. Even from several feet away, he knew she was badly hurt. John doubled his efforts, pulling himself alongside Joelle and nearly knocking over the lamp. Reaching down, he turned her face toward the light and cried out in anguish at the sight.

"Oh, Joelle! Why? Why did this happen to you?" His cries were like that of a wounded beast.

Gently, he lifted her against himself and cradled her in his arms. "Joelle, wake up, my beloved," he whispered against her ear. "Please, wake up. I love you, Joelle. Oh, how I love you."

He traced the swollen jaw and wiped at the dried blood

around her lips. "God, please help her," John begged. "Please, God. Please!"

Lillie and Daniel returned to the house to find John, holding Joelle against himself. The scene brought tears to Lillie's eyes, knowing there was nothing she could do to change the horrors of the last few hours. How was it that a single moment, a single event could so completely change the entire future?

"John, you should be in bed," Dan stated firmly. He took hold of Joelle and eased her back onto the floor. "Lillie, clear the way."

"I want to stay with her," John told his father.

Dan hoisted John to his feet and half carried, half dragged his son to the bedroom. "You can help her most by letting me work on her without interference. You aren't helping yourself or her by endangering the progress you've made. Now, do I have to sedate you to keep you here?" Daniel questioned, placing John in his bed.

"No," John answered. "I'll wait here. But, please, promise me you'll come back and tell me everything as soon as you can."

"I will," Dan promised.

By the time Dan had returned to the front room, Lillie had cleared away most of the clutter. Together they worked to treat Joelle's injured body and, much to Lillie's heartfelt sorrow, Dan confirmed her suspicions that Joelle had been raped.

The anger in Dan's voice was barely controlled. "What kind of animal does such a hideous and degrading thing?"

"Poor baby," Lillie said, brushing back dark brown ringlets from Joelle's face. "She's just a little girl, Dan."

"I know, Lillie. I know." He reached out and touched his wife's cheek. "We're going to see her through this," he told her.

"She saved John's life and mine," Lillie stated with a wavering voice. "Oh, Dan, we all might be dead but for Joelle's sacrifice."

"Let's put her to bed," Dan said softly. "You, too," he added, pulling Lillie to her feet. "You've been through too much as it is."

"I couldn't possibly rest. You'll need me to help you now. No doubt they'll be coming for you to help at the hospital and I'll have to care for John and Joelle without you. So you must tell me what to do and how to care for them properly," Lillie said and Dan knew that she was right.

"First, we put Joelle to bed. Then we'll wash her up and better treat the lacerations." Dan reached down and picked up Joelle as though she weighed no more than a sack of flour.

"You lead the way," he told Lillie and she quickly complied.

Lillie smoothed out the covers as Dan placed Joelle's still body onto the bed. "Bring the lamp, Lillie, and a basin of water."

Lillie left her husband and hurried to do as he asked. John called out to her, begging to know about Joelle, but Lillie could tell him nothing for fear of breaking into tears.

"I'll send your father as soon as I can," she told her son and hurried to bring Dan the water. "John's asking about her," Lillie said as though Dan could have missed the exchange of conversation just outside the door.

"I know. I'll go talk to him."

"What will you tell him?" Lillie asked, meeting her husband's eyes.

"I don't know." Dan's voice was uncharacteristically hollow. "I suppose the truth is the best."

"It'll tear him apart," Lillie murmured.

"But he'll have to be told sooner or later," Dan reasoned. "Better now, while he's expecting to hear the worst."

Dan walked from the room, leaving Lillie to care for Joelle and went to his son's bed. Sunlight was now beaming through the open window and John could tell by the gravity of his father's expression the news was not good.

"How bad is she hurt?" he questioned.

"I'm not sure," Dan replied. "She's still unconscious, but that's from a blow to the head. I don't know how bad a hit she sustained, but there doesn't seem to be a great deal of swelling. Her heart rate is strong and even, so I think she'll pull through."

John looked at his father suspiciously. "You aren't telling me everything."

"No," Dan said, bringing a chair beside the bed. Wearily, he sat down. "John, there's no easy way to tell you this and I desperately wish it weren't so."

"What is it?" John nearly yelled. "You said she was strong. Are you going to tell me now that she's not going to make it?"

"No, it's not that." Dan struggled for the right words. "Joelle wasn't just beaten."

John stared at his father for a moment. "What are you saying?" The truth of what he feared his father would reveal was starting to dawn on him. "Please, tell me you aren't saying. . ."

"John, these men were obviously animals. Joelle fought for all she was worth—"

"No!" he cried. "No! It isn't fair! She was saving my worthless life!" John pounded the mattress, while tears streamed down his face.

Dan reached out to still his son's fist. "Fair or not, what's happened has happened. Joelle is going to need you now more than ever. She's going to feel bad enough from the physical injuries she's sustained, but the emotional scars are going to run even deeper. She's not going to need someone who's going to spend his time pouting about its being his fault. She's going to need someone who can show her it doesn't matter. That she had no choice in the matter and that she's still the beautiful and loving woman that you fell in love with."

John swallowed hard and nodded. "I can do that for her. God knows what she's done for me. I love her so much, Dad. Just make her well and I'll do the rest."

"No, son," Dan said, with a shake of his head. "You and I can't do it alone. God will heal Joelle, just as He's worked to heal you."

# eight

Joelle became conscious in waves of sensation. First she smelled smoke and feared that the house was on fire. Then she struggled to move, but found her body racked with pain. Her lips refused to move as she tried to speak and she tasted blood when she tried to wet them with her tongue.

*What's wrong with me*? Joelle's mind wandered through a shadowy maze. *Why can't I open my eyes*? She tried to force her eyelids to part, but they refused to do as she willed them. A deep moaning came from somewhere inside her, but even then Joelle could not rationalize the reaction.

"Don't try to move, Joelle," the soft voice of Lillie came from somewhere overhead. "You've been hurt. Just lie still."

"John," she moaned the name. "Where is John?"

"John is all right, Joelle. You saved his life. You saved me, too."

*Saved his life? What is Lillie talking about*? Joelle's eyes opened a fraction and through the tiny slits she could barely make out Lillie's tear-streaked face.

"I hurt," Joelle murmured.

"I know. Dan left some medicine for you and I'll see to it that the pain eases. Can you swallow some liquid?"

"I think so." The words barely croaked out from her raw throat. "What happened?"

"You don't remember?" Lillie questioned in surprise. She stared down at the battered face and ached to make the swelling go away.

"No," Joelle whispered and seemed to fall back to sleep.

"It's just as well," Lillie said softly. She retrieved the medication and poured out a measure for Joelle. Lifting the young woman's head just a bit caused Joelle to awaken again.

"Lillie?"

"Here, just drink this. It will make you feel better."

Joelle did as she was told and fell back to sleep. Somewhere in her mind she thought she heard gunfire and the raucous laughter of foul-smelling men, but then it faded and Joelle heard nothing.

⁂

It was not until the next day that Joelle truly became conscious. She opened her eyes, again finding it a pain-filled effort, but this time a tiny seed of memory came to her. She remembered a gloved hand, slamming hard against her face.

"How do you feel?" Dan's voice was soft and full of concern.

Joelle turned her head and felt the dull ache inside grow to a throb. "I hurt."

"You will for a time. We can control it, though. I have medication for you. Are you hungry?"

"No." Joelle struggled to remember something, but she could not begin to think of what it was. "I'm thirsty."

Dan nodded and poured a glass of water from a pitcher at her bedside. "Here," he said and eased his arm behind her.

Joelle drank slowly, still trying to figure out exactly what had happened. She remembered there had been something wrong. The smell of smoke came back to her. "Was there a fire?" she whispered to Dan.

"Yes, there was," he said and laid her back against the pillow. "The Commercial Hotel was burned to the ground by the *Villistas*."

"Were we there?" Joelle questioned. Her mind struggled to clear the haze.

"No," Dan replied. "Good thing, too. The *Villistas* killed several people there before setting it on fire. It's still smoldering."

"I smell it," Joelle replied.

Dan pulled out a stethoscope and leaned over Joelle. "I'm going to listen to your heart," he said softly. "Don't be afraid."

Joelle thought it strange that he would say such a thing, but when he reached for the front of her nightgown her hands instinctively shot out. "No!"

It was the one thing to trigger her memory. Someone else had reached out to her like that. Only that man had not been a doctor; his actions had been violent and ugly.

"It's all right, Joelle. It's me, Dr. Dan. I'm going to help you get better. I won't hurt you."

Joelle shook her head from side to side. The ugliness was coming back to her. She remembered the foul odor of whiskey on the breath of the men who had grabbed her. She tried to block the image of a leering grin and dark fiery eyes.

"No! No! No!" she screamed and threw herself to the far side of the bed. Crawling back away from Dan, Joelle began to cry. She was unable to stop the assault that relived itself in her mind and all she could do was cower like a frightened child.

Lillie came running at the sound of Joelle's cries. She jumped up on the bed and pulled Joelle into her arms, cradling her as a mother would a small child.

"It's all right, Joelle. Don't cry. No one will hurt you anymore." Lillie's voice soothed Joelle's anguish.

"Make them go away," Joelle moaned, with her hands to her head. "Make them go away."

"They're gone, Joelle. They can't hurt you anymore." Lillie's calm insistence caused Joelle to still.

"Are you sure they're gone?"

"Yes," Lillie whispered, "I'm sure. Dan and John and I are the only ones here and we won't let anything bad happen to you."

"I'm afraid," Joelle croaked in a barely audible voice. "I'm so afraid."

"God is your strength and salvation," Lillie whispered. "You need not fear anyone. He is with you and He will keep you from harm."

Joelle rejected the words. "No, He doesn't care. He left me alone. He doesn't care."

Lillie looked at Daniel with deep sorrow in her eyes. "He cares, Joelle. He never stopped. Please don't harden your heart. God cares."

Dan reached out to hand Lillie a glass of medicine. "Drink this, Joelle," he said, being careful not to touch her.

Joelle opened her eyes and accepted the medication gratefully. She prayed it might cause her to sleep. She prayed it would take away the horrible images in her mind.

❧

John heard the anguished cries and felt the helplessness of his situation. He could not go to her. He could not comfort her. What use was he to anyone?

"Stop feeling sorry for yourself, John Monroe." He could

hear Joelle's words as if she were standing beside him. He had given much time over to self-pity.

"I have to stop this," he said aloud. "I won't be any good to anyone if I wallow here forever."

"Did you say something, Son?" Dan came into the room with a tired look.

"I heard Joelle. How is she?"

"She's starting to remember."

John closed his eyes and clenched his jaw. If only he could help her forget her pain and sorrow. "I want to see her," John said, opening his eyes to meet his father's.

"You can't, John. She's terrified. I think it would only make matters worse."

"But she loves me and I love her. I want her to know that none of this matters. It won't change my love for her."

"Now is not the time, John. She didn't want me there. She'll only allow Lillie to touch her. You have to understand, John. Every man, even you and me. . ." He hesitated. "She can't separate us from her attackers. She can't find comfort in you right now. Give her time. You must give her time."

John rubbed his legs and thought on his father's words. "All right. . .I'll wait."

&

Dan found himself on a constant run between the hospital and his house. When he was not trying to help with the severely wounded, it seemed there were other less serious doctoring skills needed. Always someone occupied his time, until in frustration and exhaustion, he slipped away and tended to the needs of his family.

Within a day, the train arrived to bring workers bearing

Red Cross armbands and scores of white-clad nurses. Dan wondered where they had found so many people willing to volunteer for duty in the small, forsaken town. Gratefully, he relieved himself of the massive obligations and turned his affairs outside of home over to those who had come to help.

Joelle climbed out of bed on the fourth day and, although her body still ached, she said very little about her pain. In fact, she said very little of anything to anyone. Even Lillie found it difficult to draw out the tiniest detail and rarely did Joelle even seem to notice when Lillie spoke directly to her.

It was Joelle's way of dealing with her pain. She knew in full what had happened that night and it was hard enough to come to terms with it, much less to talk about it.

John had pleaded to see her, but Joelle had refused. How could she face him now? She was soiled and used by others. She would never again be John's beloved and she wanted nothing to do with anything that would remind her of her loss. That was the reason she began to plan how she would leave. Somehow and by some means, she had to leave Columbus and get as far from John and his parents as she possibly could. Only then, she reasoned, would the demons leave her mind. Only then, would she be free from the memories.

"Joelle?" Lillie questioned, coming cautiously into the room with a tray of food. "I've brought you lunch."

"I don't want it," Joelle replied flatly.

"You need to eat. It will help you heal."

Joelle shot her a look of disbelief and then quickly turned away. "Just leave it, then."

Lillie put the tray on the bedside table and went to sit

beside Joelle. "You know I love you as a daughter, Joelle," she began. "I just want to help you through this. You've done so much for John and for Dan and me. Please let us help you."

"There's nothing you can do," Joelle stated simply, refusing to look at Lillie.

Lillie reached out and touched Joelle's hand. "When I was around your age, I lost my first husband and the child we were expecting in a tragic accident. I thought God the most cruel and inhumane Being. I railed against Him and felt that He, above all others, knew nothing of my pain. But I was wrong, Joelle. It was through my pain and that tragedy that I met Dan. He too, had his own pains from the past. He had lost a wife in childbirth and was also very angry at God."

Joelle pulled back her hand. "I'm sorry for your losses, but it has nothing to do with me."

"It does in a way," Lillie replied softly. "You've lived through a hideous nightmare. You feel that God has shown you all manner of cruelty and punishment. But He hasn't, Joelle. He hasn't sought to harm you and you mustn't turn away from Him now."

Joelle's eyes blazed. "I didn't turn away from Him, Lillie. He cast me aside. The night he allowed those men...," her words fell into a void of silence. "He threw me away," Joelle finally said.

"No, He didn't." Lillie struggled for just the right words. "We often go through bad things, but not because of God. We are as wheat being sifted...being made pure. The bad with the good, you might say, and from both we grow and learn how to cope with the challenges of life. The evil in this world, those men, and their sinful natures caused this, not God."

Joelle got to her feet. "Please go, Lillie. I just want to be alone."

"John's asking to see you. He loves you so much."

"He won't love me when he knows the truth," Joelle stated with hollow eyes staring blankly at Lillie.

"He knows the truth, Joelle."

Lillie's words hit Joelle as though she had been slapped. "He knows?" Her voice was small and weak.

"Yes, and he loves you even more. He knows that what happened to you, happened because you were saving his life. Oh, child, he knows what they did and it breaks his heart. But not because he thinks you are less than what you were, but because you think you are less than what he could love."

Joelle's eyes rimmed with tears. "He'd come to hate me."

"Never!" Lillie declared. "He could never hate you."

"Please, just go. Tell him to forget me. Tell him I release him from the obligation of our engagement. It's what he wanted before the attack. Now I see the wisdom of it."

"No, Joelle. John doesn't want to lose you. He never wanted that."

"He just feels sorry for me, like he feared I felt for him."

"Joelle," Lillie tried to speak.

Joelle just shook her head. "Please, just leave me alone."

When Lillie was gone, Joelle sat back down and stared at the food on the tray. Food, water, air to breath. How simple it all seemed. The basic requirements to keep a human body alive. But what of the spirit? What of the heart and soul of a person? What could raise those from the dead, when murder had been committed against them?

"Joelle!"

Joelle's eyes tightened shut and her hand went to her throat at the sound of John, calling her name. He kept doing that. Kept calling to her. Kept declaring his love and begging her to come to him.

"Joelle, I love you! Please don't stop loving me!"

Joelle felt the hot tears slide down her cheeks. "I'll never stop loving you, John. But, I can't be your wife," she whispered. "You deserve someone pure and that can never be me."

⧫

After Lillie left the house to take supper to Dan at the hospital, Joelle grabbed what few things she could handle and left the house. She had no idea where she would go or how she would make her way from Columbus. All she knew was that she could no longer bear to hear John's pleading voice.

She left a simple note, explaining her undying gratitude and love, with emphasis for John that her heart would forever belong to him alone. She pleaded for understanding and hoped that in time, John's pain would pass and that he would love another.

Lillie found the note upon her return and with tears in her eyes, took it to her son. "She's gone," she stated simply and handed John the letter.

He scanned it quickly. "Go find Dad. Get him to send out a search for her. She can't be far. We have to bring her back."

Lillie nodded. "If you think it best, I will. But, John, what if Joelle only hates us for interfering?"

"She can get as angry and hateful as she likes," John declared. "I owe her that, given what I put her through. Just go quickly, Mom. We can't waste any time." Lillie nodded and hurriedly left the room to retrieve Dan.

John eased his weight to the side of the bed. *Useless things,* he thought, pounding his hands against his still-weak legs. *If only I could walk, I could go after her myself,* he thought. But no, he could not even get off the bed without help. Here he was in a land he did not know well, with the love of his life fleeing from him and no way to go to her.

"Oh, God," he whispered, "if only You would heal me and let me walk. If only You would give me the power to go after her."

Outside his open window, John heard the haunting strains of a Spanish melody. The guitar's rich strings poured out the accompaniment of the once-popular *"La Golondrina"*— "The Swallow."

The Spanish words drifted up to pierce John's heart. He easily translated them and the realization of Joelle's flight was brought home in ineffable irony.

> "Where will she go, swift and weary,
> The swallow that leaves from here?
> But if in the country you strayed
> Seeking shelter and unable to find it!
> Next to my bed I will place her nest,
> In which she can spend the season. . .
> I, too, am in the lost land:
> Oh! *Cielo santo! Y sin poder volar!*"

Oh! Heaven! And unable to fly!

# nine

Joelle had no means to escape Columbus and so, in desperation, she snuck aboard a freight car when the opportunity presented itself. The train moved out of Columbus, leaving behind scores of national newspapermen and an ever-growing command of soldiers. Joelle had heard it rumored, while waiting for the train, that President Wilson was sending troops out after Pancho Villa and his men. She silently hoped the army would slaughter all of them.

It was easy to slip onto the train. No one paid her any attention and, without regard to her own safety, Joelle threw herself into the back of a halfway empty car and settled down for the ride. She fell asleep and in such complete exhaustion found the first peace she had known in days. She was still bruised and aching from her ordeal, but her real pain was emotional. The never-ending bombardment of nightmares usually allowed her little escape from her memories. Gratefully, she succumbed to the rocking motion of the train car, finally realizing that she no longer cared if she lived or died.

When she woke up, Joelle adjusted her eyes to the darkness. Somewhere along the way, someone had closed the freight car door, leaving it pitch black inside. At first it frightened her and then, feeling that nothing else could hurt her more than she had already been hurt, Joelle eased her body into a sitting position and waited for the train to reach its unknown destination.

She thought of John. She could not help it. Somehow she knew that no matter where she went, she would always think of John. She remembered with fondest memories his laughing eyes and quick wit. She even smiled at the memory of their arguments. John was so good and loving. She could only hope that the woman he one day married would be worthy of him.

"Let him marry and be happy, God," she whispered the prayer, then started at the thought of talking to God. Had she not concluded that God no longer listened to her?

_I'm listening, Joelle._

It was not an audible voice, but Joelle heard it, nevertheless.

"But You left me alone!" Joelle declared.

_Never, my child._

Joelle felt the train slowing and whether it was due to a planned stop or merely the obligation of an upcoming town, Joelle prepared herself to exit the car.

The train groaned to a stop and although Joelle had no idea where she had arrived, she thrust her full weight against the door and managed to open it enough to jump to the ground.

It was dark outside and cold. Colder than she had remembered in Columbus. But then, in Columbus she had never before ventured outside in the dead of night.

There was a small train depot and a smattering of people milling around the train engine. Joelle crept silently to the side of the depot and down the sandy roadway. She passed by several darkened adobe buildings. They seemed oblivious to her plight in their orange-brown silence.

The moonlight overhead did little to aid her journey and finally Joelle sat down against the side of a small building and considered what she should do. The town seemed quite inhospitable at the lateness of the hour and Joelle began to wonder if she should just seek out the nearest telegraph and wire her parents.

"No, I can't go home to them. I can't go home until I know," she whispered to herself. A frightening question had risen up to haunt Joelle and she desperately desired to have it answered before she made any plans for her future.

"You'll freeze out here, child," the voice was gentle, ancient, and kind.

Joelle would have jumped at the sound of the voice, but her weariness of spirit gave her no reason to care. She gazed up into the face of an elderly man, a priest it seemed from the look of his clothing.

"I'll be fine," she answered and clutched her bag for warmth.

"I dreamed of a lamb, caught in a snare," the white-haired man replied as though Joelle had remained silent. "It was so real that I had to come check."

"Did you find one?" Joelle asked innocently.

The man's wrinkled face broke into a smile. "I believe I have."

Joelle felt immediately at ease. "I'm no lamb, but I suppose you could say I'm caught in a snare."

"Come along, little one. These old bones won't take the desert cold. I have a fire and a room that will serve you well. Rise up and come with me."

Joelle stared at him in mute surprise. His words were so like those of John's when he had quoted Song of Solomon.

Struggling against the need for comfort and the desire to fade into oblivion, Joelle got to her feet and sighed.

"I suppose it would be nice to get warm."

The priest nodded and began to walk. "I am Father Cooper and I watch over the flock of this tiny parish."

"I'm Joelle Dawson." She offered nothing more and the man seemed satisfied to leave it at that.

He motioned to the adobe dwelling that rested behind a small church. "It isn't a mansion, but it manages to meet my needs."

"It looks fine," Joelle said and followed him into the house.

A warm fire did indeed glow out from the domelike fireplace in the corner of the main room. Joelle gazed longingly at its cheery flames.

"Go ahead, child. Warm yourself," the ancient priest invited.

Joelle hurried to the structure, dropped her bag, and held out her stiffened fingers. "It feels wonderful," she said softly.

"Are you hungry?"

Joelle could not ignore the rumbling of her stomach. She could not even remember when she had eaten a proper meal. "Yes," she replied, "I suppose I am."

"I have some beans and tortillas left over from supper. Would you care to partake of it?" He watched Joelle intently for her answer.

"I would be very grateful," Joelle replied.

"Then I will fetch it from the stove. You sit there by the fire, while I see to it."

Joelle watched Father Cooper go from the room. He seemed to be one of those antiquated characters from the previous century and Joelle instantly liked him. It was funny, she thought. It seemed very right and good to be under his care. Yet, here was a total stranger, a man whom for all she knew could very well be no different from those who had harmed her.

"You have traveled far, yes?" he questioned, returning with a plate of food. His voice held the slightest hint of an accent.

"I don't really know," Joelle replied. "I'm not sure where I am, but I caught the train in Columbus."

"Then you have come about forty miles north, northeast," Father Cooper replied. "I see you are injured," he motioned to her face. "Were you there during the attack on the city?"

Joelle's countenance darkened. "Yes."

The one-word reply left Father Cooper little doubt that she did not wish to discuss the matter further. He watched as she ate in silence and when she had cleaned the contents of the plate, he got to his feet.

"Your room is over here," he stated and picked up the bag she had left by the fire. "Please, light a candle for yourself. You will find them in the box by the door."

Joelle did as he instructed and followed him down a short hallway. Father Cooper opened the door to a tiny room. There was a single, old-fashioned bed in one corner and a cross on the wall. Joelle noted the furnishings with a heart of gladness. It was safe and warm and away from the painful memories of Columbus.

"It is small, yes, but it is yours."

"Thank you," Joelle murmured.

"God bless you, child. Sleep well. We will talk in the morning," Father Cooper said, closing the door as he took his leave.

Joelle did not even undress. She put the candle on the

sawed-off frame of the bed and sat down wearily. The bed sagged, betraying the roping that held the thinly stuffed mattress, but Joelle did not care. She blew out the candle, slipped off her shoes, and fell back against the scratchy woolen blanket.

The nightmares came, as they did most every time she slept. Joelle relived the anguish of her rape, over and over, with every dream. She could hear their laughter, feel their breath against her face. Always she would wake up in a cold sweat, unable to shake the feeling of being hit and mauled. Pulling her knees to her chest, Joelle clutched them tightly and squeezed her eyes shut. When would the images leave her? When would she ever be free?

·≥·

After a restless night, morning came and with it, the delicious aroma of sausage frying. Joelle jumped from the bed, sought out her brush, and quickly rebraided her hair. She thought for a moment about changing her clothes, then decided against it. If she had to travel again today, she might as well wear the same old things.

"Good morning," she said shyly, entering Father Cooper's kitchen.

"Ah, so you are awake. I have begun the breakfast. Will you join me?"

Joelle smiled at the sight of the little man, working his way along the stove and counter, to prepare his fare. "I would be grateful."

Father Cooper motioned her to the cupboard. "There are dishes in there and cups. We will have hot tea with our sausage and eggs."

Joelle went to the cupboard and pulled down two plates

and matching cups. They were an ancient pattern of a once-fashionable china set. She thought how like Father Cooper the dishes were. Castoffs from another time and place, yet still serviceable.

She set the table and clasped her hands together, wishing she knew something to say. Father Cooper brought the skillet and all to the table. Joelle peered inside to see the concoction of eggs and sausage all scrambled together.

"It looks delicious," she said, offering the slightest smile.

Father Cooper blessed the meal and offered Joelle a seat, before taking one opposite her at the tiny table. "We are a poor people here, but the Lord does provide, *oui*?"

"You're French," Joelle said in surprise.

"But of course," the man replied as though she should not have been surprised. Joelle smiled, but made no further comment.

"You are traveling to your home?" Father Cooper asked.

"No," Joelle said, shaking her head. She pushed around the food on her plate, spooning in several bites, trying to think of what to say next. "I guess I have no home," she finally managed.

"You are alone?"

"Yes," she replied. Then to the old man's delight, she added in French. "I'm without family or funds and seek refuge and work. Would you have knowledge of someone nearby, who might need my assistance?"

"I have not heard my language spoken in a very long time," Father Cooper replied with a smile of sheer pleasure breaking the wrinkled paths around his mouth. "I believe I can help you. I could not pay you, but you could live here and share meals with me."

"What would I do?"

"You could gather wood for my fire and keep my house and garden," he offered.

"I can also cook. I know several wonderful French recipes," Joelle beamed at the man, with sudden interest in his suggestion.

"It would be to my delight, Joelle Dawson."

"Very well," she said, feeling great relief to have the matter resolved. "I will stay for a time with you, Father Cooper, and share your hospitality."

"You will share also your heartache, no?"

Joelle started at his words. She put down her fork and stared thoughtfully at her plate. She had no reason to fear this man or his condemnation. He was a man of God and the loving kindness that he had already extended to her gave Joelle no reason to doubt his earnest concern.

"I will share what I can," Joelle replied softly. She looked up with wide, dark eyes to see the compassion in the aged face that looked back at her. "It is a great burden that I bear and I'm uncertain that if shared it will be any lighter."

"All burdens shared make lighter the load. It is less work when two carry the water, instead of one."

Joelle nodded and looked back at her food. "Perhaps."

# ten

"But Joelle won't come back to Bandelero!" John protested. Once again he was under the roof of his parents, only this time things were much different. He was no longer the young naive boy who had gone off to join the army. Now he was a cripple, or nearly that, and hopelessly worried about the whereabouts of the woman he wanted to marry.

"Well, she certainly wasn't coming back to Columbus," Lillie stated, pushing John's wheelchair to one side. Squeezing past her son's intentional roadblock, Lillie paused to give John's shoulder a pat. "Get well first, then worry about finding her. Joelle will either come back here or go home to her parents. She won't wander around forever."

"I don't like the idea of her wandering around out there at all. I want her here, where I can take care of her."

"I beg your pardon?" Lillie said, looking down at her son. "You have a great deal of healing to do yourself, John. How can you concentrate on caring for Joelle when you need to work on putting yourself back together?"

John shook his head and ran his fingers back through his hair. "I know you're right. But. . ."

"But?"

"I need her. She makes me feel alive. Even when she was arguing with me, I wanted to laugh with her, hold her, love her. She's got to understand that what happened in Columbus isn't important to me, at least not in a way that matters about my feelings for her. If anything, I just love her more. She said that anything was preferable to letting me die. I feel anything is preferable to going through life without her."

Lillie's face softened. "I know, John. Give it over to God. He knows where she is and He can lead her home."

John nodded and wheeled himself off to his bedroom. His father had redone the bedroom to accommodate John's various needs and, closing the door behind him, John prayed that wherever she was, someone would meet Joelle's needs, as well.

He noticed the papers still lying on the dresser and moved the chair closer to retrieve them. They were his discharge orders and although he knew it had to be that way, John felt as though a major part of his life was over.

He closed his eyes and could almost feel himself back in the cockpit of the Jenny. If desire and will could make it so, John would have already been flying again, flying and soaring high above the turmoil and unrest of the earth.

For several minutes he sat there motionless, seeing in his mind the graceful plane as she glided across the sky. It would never be his again, he thought silently.

"But at least it was mine for a time," he murmured. He needed to be glad for the time he had enjoyed as a pilot. Some folks never had a chance to enjoy what they really and truly loved.

A knock at his bedroom door ended John's dreams for the moment. "Come in."

Lillie appeared and on her face was a strained look. "John, Joelle's parents are here. Would you mind talking with them?"

John shook his head. "I don't mind." He tossed the papers aside and wheeled his chair to the door. "Just lead the way."

Riley and Zandy Dawson were sitting stiffly, with grim expressions lining their faces. Riley got to his feet and extended his hand to John.

"It's been a long time, but I do believe we met at Christmas, after my son, Nicholas, married Daughtry Lucas."

"Yes, I remember that well," John replied. "How are you Mr. Dawson, Mrs. Dawson?"

"Please, just call me Riley," Joelle's dark-haired father requested. He reclaimed his seat beside his wife and John became acutely aware of how much Joelle resembled him.

"And you must call me Zandy," the brown-haired woman at his side stated.

John noticed the soft touches of gray that peppered Riley's hair while, except for the lines of worry, Zandy Dawson seemed hardly older than her daughter. He smiled sadly. "I'm sorry we couldn't get together under better circumstances. I'd figured on us getting under one roof for a wedding this spring."

"We'd heard about that possibility," Riley said, as though he had not been entirely sure of the matter.

John folded his hands in his lap. "I love her very much."

Zandy leaned forward to cover John's hands with one of her own. She said nothing, but her eyes met his with an all-telling look.

"We're staying with Garrett and Maggie Lucas," Riley said, breaking the tense silence.

"I presumed you might be," Lillie said before John could reply. "Dan says that Daughtry's baby is due just about any day."

"We're quite excited," Zandy replied. "If only. . ." She grew quiet and eased back against the sofa.

" 'If onlys' don't get us very far," John whispered, remembering his mother's words. "I'm full of those and they haven't served me well."

"Do you have any news at all?" Riley questioned.

"No," John answered. "Nothing. I put friends to work on it down in Columbus, but the army's kind of got their hands full with tracking down Villa. My brother, J.D., is searching for Joelle in El Paso—"

"Why there?" Zandy interrupted to ask.

"It was close and a pretty good size of town. We figured she might have gone there just to lose herself in the crowds for a while," Lillie replied.

"She couldn't have gotten far," John added. "She didn't have much cash with her."

"I see," Riley shifted uncomfortably and shot a quick glance at his wife. "I'm going to hire some men to look for her. We'll start in Columbus and work from there."

"As soon as I'm out of this thing, I plan to go after her myself," John said in a voice that betrayed his frustration.

"We know you will," Zandy said, hoping to give him comfort.

"We'll be at the ranch if you get any news," Riley continued. "I understand they still don't have a telephone, but I'll ride in here daily to check with you. If you don't mind, I'll give my men this number, as well."

"Of course," Lillie stated. "You're welcome to stay here, you know, but I'm sure you'll want to be near Daughtry and Nick."

Riley and Zandy nodded and got to their feet. "We'd better head back," Riley said and extended his hand to John.

"We'll find her, keep the faith. God hasn't brought us all this far, just to desert us."

John nodded and watched his mother walk them to the door. He felt even more useless, thinking of how he must have appeared to them. With renewed spirit, John was more determined than ever to get back on his feet. *If my life has to change, let it. But let me have some form of control over it*, he thought.

❧

April brought the birth of Heidi Dawson. At seven and one-half pounds, she was healthy and strong, for which everyone sincerely thanked God. Daughtry and Nicholas, ever the proud parents, were joyful in their new arrival. Kent, Heidi's older brother who was not quite two, did not know what he thought of the squalling baby.

"Bebe," he said, pointing an accusing finger.

"That's right, my boy," Nicholas said, holding Kent close enough to touch his new sister. "That's your baby sister, Heidi."

"I. . .D." Kent tried his version of the name.

"That's right," Daughtry said from her bed. "Later we'll let you hold her."

"Did you give her a middle name?" Riley asked from where he stood with Zandy. They proudly shared the laurels of grandparents with Maggie and Garrett Lucas.

"Joelle," Daughtry stated softly. "Her name is Heidi Joelle."

Zandy's eyes filled with tears and Riley pulled her close. "That's beautiful, Daughtry. Thank you. I'm sure Joelle will be honored."

"We hope so," Daughtry said, glad for Nicholas's supportive hand, now resting on her shoulder. "Joelle was. . .is a great comfort to us."

Maggie came forward to take Kent from his father. "I think it's somebody's bedtime."

"No nap! No nap!" Kent chanted and could be heard all the way down the hall.

"I think I'll give your mother a hand," Daughtry's bearded father said. "If you'll excuse me."

When Daughtry's parents had gone, Nicholas noticed the worried look his parents exchanged. "Has there been any word?" he asked.

"No, nothing," Riley answered and pulled Zandy with him to Daughtry's bedside.

"Poor Joelle," Daughtry whispered. "She had to bear so much. I've prayed constantly for her."

"So have we," Zandy admitted to her daughter-in-law. The dejection was clear in her voice. "It's so hard to just stand by and wait. Sometimes I get so angry at her. She knows the torment she's putting us through. She couldn't possibly be unaware of the pain we're suffering."

"She's not aware," Daughtry said firmly. "I'm certain of that. She was always very concerned about you both, when she was staying with Nicholas and me. I'm sure it's just that her own sorrows are so great, she can't think beyond them."

"That's why she should come home," Riley retorted.

"That's why she should," Nicholas offered in reply, "but it's also why she won't."

❧

Joelle sat quietly knitting, while Father Cooper strained against the poor light and his own thick spectacles to read a lengthy letter. Putting aside her work, Joelle went to where he sat.

"Would you like for me to read it?"

Father Cooper surrendered the papers to her youthful hands. "It would greatly please these weary eyes, if you would be so kind."

Joelle read him the letter, a missive from a brother in the service. The shaky handwriting was nearly as poor as that of Father Cooper's and Joelle deemed them to be contemporaries in age. By the time she finished with the correspondence, Father Cooper sat dozing in his chair.

Joelle smiled and leaned back to close her own eyes. She had been Father Cooper's house guest for nearly two and one-half months. It had been most difficult at first, but he had quickly disarmed her fears with his zany tales of France in his boyhood and how he had nearly gotten kicked out of the seminary for putting alum in the drinking water. He was quite a character, her Father Cooper, and Joelle was very grateful to have made his acquaintance.

She was also grateful for the friendship he had extended. He never pressured her for answers that she found impossible to give and he always seemed to understand when her sorrows kept her silent and unresponsive.

Joelle ran her hand lightly across her abdomen and thought of the child who grew there. She now had the answer to that frightful question. She would give birth to a child in December. She grimaced and opened her eyes. What kind of child could possibly come from such a union? This baby was conceived in violence and rage. What possible good could come from that?

Joelle tried to shake the image that always flooded her thoughts. It was the picture of a monstrously deformed and hideous creature being placed in her arms. Her child, she thought. . .and she reasoned, her punishment.

# eleven

With the use of a cane, John limped across the floor. The broad grin on his face was directed at the two men who stood at the opposite side of the room. The first was his Uncle David, the second was his father.

"I'm almost as good as new," John said, sweat beading his forehead.

"I knew if anyone could do it, you could," Daniel told his son.

"You've got your father's determination," David said with a laugh. "And, it's done you well."

"I'd imagine those prayers you had your congregation saying for me didn't hurt, Uncle David."

David nodded. "You bet they didn't." After over twenty years of pastoring the largest church in Bandelero, David definitely believed in the power of prayer.

"So now what are you going to do?" Dan questioned. "As if I had to ask."

"You don't." John's face left little doubt to his plan. "I'm going after her."

"You can't overdo it, even now. You'll tire easier than before and if you sit a horse very long, you'll spend the following days nursing your aches and pains."

"I'm going after her," John said firmly. "And when I find her, I'm going to marry her on the spot before she can get away from me again."

"Good for you!" David declared. "Is there anything we can do to help?"

"Keep those people praying," John replied with a grin.

"You've got it and I know God is working through the details, as we speak."

John limped to the door. "I'm going to get my things ready. I've got a train to catch."

"John," Dan said, coming beside his son. "Try not to expect too much at first. It has been over six months."

"You talking about my physical condition or my finding Joelle?"

"Both," Dan replied seriously.

"I'll be fine," John assured his father. "And, I will find Joelle."

⁂

Joelle enjoyed the mild October weather. She had worked outdoors in the vineyards throughout the summer months, whenever she was not helping Father Cooper. Her time spent outside had darkened her skin to a golden brown and, thankfully, she blended in quite naturally with the Mexican and Indian residents of the small village.

Carrying a load of mesquite on her head just as the other women did, Joelle looked as though she very well might be the beautiful descendent of Spanish nobility. If they only knew, she laughed to herself.

Her condition had become quite obvious and Father Cooper, sensing her need for privacy, had found Joelle a tiny adobe house near the church. Joelle repaid the owner by gathering extra firewood and taking in laundry. She would also bake bread in the *horno,* a domed-shaped, adobe oven that sat outdoors. She could not say that she was happy, but she had become complacent. She still thought of John and her parents, as well as Lillie and Dan, but the child she carried kept her from even letting them know that she was safe.

"What could I say to them?" she had said to Father Cooper one evening before supper. "John would feel obligated to make the child his own, or my parents would feel the need to shelter me and take over the task for themselves. I can't burden them like that, not even for my own comfort."

"What is it that you want, Joelle?" Father Cooper had quietly asked. They were strolling down the sandy roadway, enjoying the tapestry of colors in the autumn sunset.

Joelle had thought for a moment. "I can't tell you or you'd think me ungrateful."

"I would never think badly of you, my child."

They had walked on in silence, while Joelle struggled to come to terms with what she felt. She had stared past the ramshackle *jacales*, homes of little more than mud and wooden poles, and she had sighed. She had no words for the sorrow deep inside of her. The ineffable pain that came any time she tried to rationalize her choices caused her to distance herself from even her dear friend.

"I wish to die," she had stated simply. Snapping her head up to meet Father Cooper's eyes, she had frowned. "Does that shock you?"

"Shock me? No," Father Cooper had replied with a shake of his head. "You have borne your cross with grace, Joelle. You haven't complained or grumbled of the great injustice done you, although just that is true. However, God's Word is clear about life and death. It has never been ours to give or to take. So just as it is impossible for you to have created the life that grows inside your body, it is also quite unreasonable to imagine that you can take one day away from your life here on this earth."

"But I'm tired," Joelle had replied, allowing the weariness to creep into her voice. "I'm just getting through minute by minute, day by day. I have no will to see the future. . .no desire whatsoever to endure even another minute." She had paused for a moment. "You've been so good to me, but I need much more and there is no one who can give it. I'm alone and lonely and to face the thought of delivering this child, scares me to death."

"The place where we say our prayers may be different," Father Cooper had said in his gentle way, "even the way in which we pray, but we serve the same God. He requires only that we come unto Him. Matthew 11:28 says, ' "Come unto me, all ye that labour and are heavy laden, and I will give you rest.' " You are tired from your burden, but God will lighten it and give you rest and in rest comes strength, Joelle. Trust our Father to give you that need."

"But what of this life?" she had said with a hand upon her swollen middle.

"All life is sacred, child. Just as I said, you could no more snap your fingers and create a life, than I could."

"But people create children all the time," Joelle had said rather indignantly. "I've known of many folks who've spoken of surprises they received in children they'd not expected."

"Man and woman do not create the life. They are but the receptacles of God's gift. God creates that life. He alone has the power to breathe spirit into fresh and blood. Joelle, be reasonable and forgive me for my bluntness, but people often join together in a marriage bed and no children come forth from that union."

Joelle had thought on Father Cooper's words for a

moment. "I suppose that is true. I just never thought of it much. I guess I just imagined that husbands and wives would naturally have a child most every time they came together."

"But that is the glory of it, Joelle. It is never our decision or our predetermination. We cannot choose one time to create a life and another time to snap our fingers and choose against it. God is the One Who determines our paths. Just as He created your life, He also created the life you carry within."

"But this child was created out of sin. Out of violence and all that is unholy, this baby came into existence. How could that be something of God?" Joelle had questioned in earnest.

Father Cooper had placed his hands upon Joelle's shoulders. "My child, you may seek God in all things or you may seek the world. If you choose the world, you may find that you completely miss the blessings and wonderment of the Father's touch. And that, Joelle, is the true tragedy."

Joelle had stared back at the priest in silence. His words had pierced the hardness of her heart. Turning without a word, Joelle had begun to walk again. When they had reached her little house, Father Cooper had taken her hand and patted it ever so gently.

"God's blessings upon you, Joelle," he had said. "I am praying for you."

"Thank you," Joelle had whispered and then placed a kiss upon the weathered cheek of her friend.

❧

America moved closer to the November presidential elections with one concerned eye on the Mexican border and another poised on the war in Europe. President Wilson's campaign promoted his reelection by saying, "He kept us out of war!" People could only ask themselves, "Yes, but can he continue to do so?"

Black Jack Pershing had been called in shortly after the Villa raid on Columbus to head up the "Punitive Expedition." This affair called for three brigades, two cavalry units and one infantry, supported by field artillery, engineers, wagon companies, ambulances, and the First Air Squadron out of San Antonio, Texas. Their objective was to go after Villa and his troops. But late into 1916, Villa was still leading Pershing on a merry chase and Mexico was growing ever more angry at the U.S. invasion of their country.

Joelle heard very little of the news. She liked it that way and she never really went out of her way to learn any more than what Father Cooper shared with her. To know more only caused her to worry about those she loved. Whenever she thought of war, she remembered John and J.D., as well as Daughtry's brothers and scores of old friends from home. She hated to imagine them marching off to war and hated even more to imagine them never coming home again.

As was her routine, Joelle went to Father Cooper's little church and prepared to clean it. It was a very unassuming building of adobe with a flat roof and dirt floor. The walls were four feet thick and the windows were small but remarkably glassed with colored panes and artistry that captivated the imagination.

Inside, Joelle really had very little to do. The altar was simple, unpainted wood and it was her duty to dust it for the services to come. Before her arrival, Father Cooper generally saw to the matter himself, but Joelle wanted to make herself useful and so he conceded this task to her.

As was the custom, the church had no pews. The families

Come Away My Love 115

of the area were mainly Mexican and because of this, the men would stand and the women kneel throughout their mass. Joelle had watched the mass once and had found it most fascinating. The women while praying, crossed themselves frequently in the Spanish tradition and kissed their thumbs after each sign of the cross. She did not understand the reasons behind what the worshipers did, yet she found their sincerity and devotion admirable.

From her days spent with these women, Joelle knew she could never have asked for better neighbors or friends. She was never in want for anything, so long as someone knew she had need. Joelle had but to express a desire to Father Cooper and inevitably, some dark-eyed woman would show up on her doorstep. With a smile and a string of explanations that Joelle was only coming to understand in bits and pieces, the desired item would be deposited into her hands. It made Joelle cautious in speaking her mind, but her love of these people deepened in the face of her own adversity.

Without realizing it, Joelle also came to see that the actions of men like Villa's did not necessarily constitute the support of an entire people. Of course, she knew these people lived in the United States, but their ties were strongly and quite obviously connected to old Mexico.

Stepping into the coolness of the building, Joelle was met with a deep sense of spirituality that she had not expected. The wooden cross that graced the front of the church drew her eyes and Father Cooper's words came back to her in a rush of emotion.

The child inside her kicked hard as though compelling its mother to listen and heed the loving priest's words. "All life is sacred," Joelle remembered aloud. She ran her hand across her stomach as if noticing for the first time the way it bulged out in front of her.

"We cannot choose one time to create a life and another time to snap our fingers and choose against it. God is the One Who determines our paths. Just as He created your life, He also created the life you carry within," Father Cooper had told her.

"The child," Joelle said slowly, "this child. . .frightens me." She raised her eyes to the cross and paused to reflect on the symbol. "I don't know what to do. I don't know whether to go home or stay here and bear this shame alone. I don't know what to do."

Tears began to fall down her cheeks and Joelle felt as though her legs could no longer support her weight. Going to the altar, she came to her knees and sobbed. "This is my fate, my destiny. But, God, what of Your Will? What of Your protection and comfort and," Joelle paused to take a ragged breath, "and love? What of Your love? How can I find it in this?"

She gripped the altar and pleaded for direction. "Show me what to do. I have no one."

As if a warm blanket had been placed around her shoulders, Joelle felt the presence of God's love surround her. There was no immediate revelation. No simple answer to guide her in the complexities of life's mysteries. It was just a quietness of spirit that descended into her heart and gave her peace.

"I will do what You guide me to do," she whispered.

Getting to her feet, Joelle stared out across the room and startled when a flash of three gruesome faces came to haunt her memory.

*Forgove them*, a still, small voice told her heart.

"Never!" she said with a shake of her head. Looking back to the cross, she was still shaking her head. "You ask too much."

## twelve

John's arrival into Columbus, New Mexico was considerably calmer than the one he had made back in January. He was overwhelmed with the sights that greeted him and realized just how few memories he had made in the small community. Most of his time had been confined to bed and, outside of Joelle's lengthy descriptions of her day or his mother's prattling about her shopping ordeals, John had not seen much at all.

His first order of business was to go to the headquarters at Camp Furlong. He had friends there and knew, too, that it was here he would get his best information.

Leaving his bag at the train station, John limped slowly through the sandy street. His destination was less than a block from the depot, but the sand made his progress difficult. John knew better than to curse his condition. He was quite grateful for the progress he had made. Even though he could not walk with ease and might never again walk without a cane, he was happy just to be on his own two feet.

At the camp headquarters John introduced himself and was soon directed to the officers' mess shack, where he was told he could find one of the commanding officers. A brief discussion with the officer in charge resulted in John's being given a place to bed down and the news that his friend, Flipflop, was quartered nearby.

"Private Campbell is working behind the stables," the

officer instructed. "We have some problems back there and I'm certain you'll find yourself quite interested."

"Thank you for your help, sir," John said, raising his hand to salute. The habit died at midpoint, as John remembered he was no longer a part of this life and its requirements.

John limped silently from the tent. His leg was hurting him and the aching in his back had grown from a tolerable dullness to a dedicated throbbing. Still, he moved on and prayed for the strength to continue.

Past the long row of stables, John could already make out the structured frames of biplanes. His breath caught and his chest tightened as he cleared the last obstacle and stood in full view of the airfield.

This had been his world and he had loved it more than most anything else in his life. He loved the droning noise and the oily smell of the engines. He cherished the feel of exhilaration when, after a jolting run down the sandy runway, the Jenny would lift herself into the air and blow a kiss goodbye to the ground below. Then of course, there was the flight itself. The feeling of being above all the mundane and routine things of the world. The feeling that in flight, one came just a little bit closer to God.

John shuddered the images away. It was no longer his world. Never again would he work the rudders or feel the stick in his hand. It was someone else's world now.

"That you, Preacher?" the voice called out from somewhere to John's right.

Turning, John spied Flipflop and grinned. "So they promoted you to corporal? Who did you have to pay off to get that?"

Flipflop laughed and double-timed his steps to give John a bear hug. "It is you. I thought I'd never see you again.

You back to join us?"

John shook his head and nearly moaned under the strength of Flipflop's embrace. He set the younger man away from him and eyed him carefully. "Those days are over for me." He held up the cane. "This is the only stick I get to handle now."

Flipflop sobered with a nod. "I heard they mustered you out. Heard, too, that you'd never walk again, but here you are."

John smiled. "Just as stubborn as I ever was." He looked beyond Flipflop and motioned to the Jennys. "So why are they on the ground?"

"We're in bad shape, Preacher. Those machines just can't tolerate what the army wants to put them through. We've messed around with the loads. We've given her more power and trimmed down her weight, but the air is too dry here, the sand too harsh. Why, there've been storms that ripped holes the size of baseballs in her fabric. I have to wonder if we'll ever get it right."

"Oh, they'll get it right. Flight is going to forever change the military, you just wait and see. Once someone figures out how to give us an air machine with enough power to go the distance and carry the loads, you'll see wars ending overnight. Why just look at what they're doing with them in France. Some good American pilots are over there flying in their corps."

"I know you're right, Preach," Flipflop replied, "but, down here, we just ain't havin' much luck. They try to put up a few planes to figure out where the *Villistas* are and inevitably they get knocked back down. We've lost quite a few to sand storms and such and at five-thousand dollars a machine, I don't think the army's real eager to keep it up."

John stared thoughtfully across the field. He could see it all in the future. Row after row of airplanes, lined up, waiting for their duties. Flipflop could see only the frustrations of the early years at hand, but John knew there was a bigger picture that stretched beyond the problems of the present.

"Say," Flipflop said with a sudden revelation, "I had a letter from J.D. the day before yesterday. His unit has joined Pershing in pursuit of Villa. Did you know that?"

"No, I haven't heard from J.D. in some time. I suppose he'll write to Mom and Dad about it, but in case he doesn't, why don't you fill me in on it and I'll send them the news."

John learned all that he could about his brother, then shared his search for Joelle with his friend. He left nearly a half-hour later, feeling somewhat better for the renewal of his friendship, yet no closer to knowing the whereabouts of Joelle.

❧

For the next few days, John paced out every square foot of Columbus. He asked questions of everyone and showed Joelle's photograph to anyone who would stop long enough to look. No one had seen the dark-eyed young woman.

Stopping at the bank, John questioned the tellers and even requested to speak with the man in charge, before he felt satisfied that Joelle had not come there to receive money. He moved around to the businesses, always receiving the same shake of the head and negative response. In complete dejection, John decided to leave Columbus and work his way along with the rail lines.

He reasoned that perhaps Joelle had managed to keep aside enough money to take the train from Columbus. He questioned the ticket agent at the train station, but the man could scarcely be held to account for the purchase of tickets way back in March. He had not even held the job then and was of no help to John. Buying a ticket, John felt utter hopelessness engulf him. His father had told him not to expect too much; after all Joelle's own father had hired professional men to search for her. The police were notified throughout the state of her disappearance and her photograph had been hand carried to law enforcement people in all the surrounding large cities. If all of these people combined could not locate her, how could John expect to pull off the deed?

The train took him east and when John realized that he had learned very little pursuing the matter in this manner, he got off at the first small town and went in search of a horse.

"This horse is a fine animal, *señor*," the dark-skinned man told John. "He is very gentle," the man added, noting John's cane.

"I'll take him," John replied and began bartering for a saddle.

The man counted out his money, while John saddled his new acquisition. He glanced up from his task to look around the small town.

"I'm looking for a young woman," he said to the man. "She's my fiancée, actually. We were separated after a tragedy and I'm afraid she might be lost and not know how to get back home."

"Who is this woman?"

John left the horse and brought out his photograph of Joelle. "Ahh, she is *muy bonito*," the man said, noting Joelle's beauty. "But, I have not seen this woman."

"If she were here, would you know it?"

"*Sí*, we are a very small village here," the man replied. "There are no strangers."

"I understand," John said and tucked the photograph back into his pocket.

Within the hour, John was back on his way and although he had to rest often and had found the ride most challenging, he strengthened his mind with the hope of finding Joelle.

After a week of searching and spending his nights out on the open desert plains, John was ready for a hot bath and a hotel bed. The desert was a harsh companion even in this late time of the year. He was constantly eating and wearing more sand than he had ever imagined existed and he had run-ins with several rattlesnakes, making his horse a most unhappy companion. Wearily, John made his way to Las Cruces, the largest city in the area, and prayed he might find someone, anyone, who had seen his beloved, Joelle. If nothing else, however, he would rest here and regain his strength.

He was still some miles away from the town, when up ahead he spotted an automobile. A wizened old man stood staring down questioningly, when John came abreast of the vehicle.

John immediately recognized the man as a priest and slowed his mount. "Good afternoon."

"Good afternoon to you," the man said with a smile.

"Having trouble with your car?" John questioned, gingerly getting down from his horse. He pulled out his cane from where the old-timers might have carried a rifle, and limped to where the old man stood.

"It seems I have managed to get off the road and the sand has quite inconveniently trapped me here."

John sized up the situation. "I think between me and my horse, we can pull you out of this spot. By the way," John straightened and extended his hand. "I'm John. . .John Monroe."

"I am Father Cooper," the old man said. "I was on my way to Las Cruces. I must make the trip periodically," he added as an explanation. "I borrow this automobile, the only one in our village, for the journey and up until this day, I have never had any problem with it. But now, alas, you see it is no longer so."

"Well, it won't cause you a problem for long," John said assuringly.

It took only a few minutes to free the vehicle and Father Cooper was most delighted. "I thank God for sending you my way, son," he said with a beaming face that John could not help but like. "Where are you bound now?"

"I'm going to Las Cruces," John replied. "I've been out here over a week and I'm stiff and sore. I was injured several months ago and I'm still not able to get around like I used to. I find myself in need of a little recuperative time."

"Perhaps you would ride the rest of the way with me?" Father Cooper suggested. "The car is surely more comfortable than your mount and I would be happy to have you share supper with me."

John nodded. "That sounds mighty good to me."

Father Cooper moved to open the car door. "If I might impose upon you to give the car a crank, we can be on our way."

"Just let me tie the horse to the back," John replied and went to the task.

"Is the switch on?" John called as he bent to crank life into the machine.

"Yes," Father Cooper called back.

John felt the ache in his back intensify, but nonetheless saw to his duty. The engine sputtered to life with Father Cooper adjusting the throttle as John joined him. Easing into the padded seat, John sighed. Yes, this was much easier to tolerate than the rigid stiffness of the saddle. As soon as they began the bouncing ride into town, however, John was not all that sure the trade-off had been a positive one.

The twin towers of St. Genevieve's Church soon came into view with the rest of the rambling town of Las Cruces. The church was a massive, brick structure patterned after the Gothic-French revival style. It was an overpowering sight that commanded the attention of anyone who looked upon it. John felt hope in the sight of the crosses that graced the double peaks of the bell towers.

"Over there is the Loretto Academy," Father Cooper commented, steering the car around a massive hole in the road. "The Sisters run a school there and have an excellent music department. They assure me they are quite modern, whatever that means."

John smiled and resumed his survey of the city. There were more trees here and the desert seemed less oppressive. Cottonwoods and numerous orchard trees dotted the banks of the Rio Grande and in the background the silhouetted Organ Mountains, so named for their pipe organ appearance, rose in shadowy black against the pink and purple twilight.

"They have completed a dam at Elephant Butte," Father Cooper was saying. "It has helped to make the area water more predictable. They no longer worry so about the flood or drought and the crops they grow are magnificent. Such alfalfa as you have never seen!"

John only nodded. They drove past the traditional adobe homes, with John noting a few houses built of brick or stone. He was grateful to see the word "hotel" labeling the tops of more than one building and sighed to himself in anticipation of his rest.

"Why don't you join me," Father Cooper said, pulling the car alongside an iron fence. "I am certain there is room for you to stay with me tonight."

"I couldn't impose," John answered.

"There will be no imposition. Come along, we will have supper and talk."

John felt there was little to do but follow the old man.

They settled in to a hearty meal of stewed meat and vegetables, with a young boy running back and forth to see to their needs. At one point he brought out huge loaves of fresh, white bread that caused John's mouth to water instantly. Father Cooper was treated royally and there was no question of John's ability to stay, when the elderly man made the request.

"So you are traveling with a purpose, no?" the priest asked.

John grinned. "You might say that."

"And you will share that purpose with me?"

"Might as well. I share it with most everyone I meet," John replied in between bites of food. He shifted his weight in the chair and grimaced.

"Are your injuries causing you great difficulty?" Father Cooper asked softly.

"I'm pretty sore. It's just as well, though," John said and paused to straighten his aching back. "Months ago, I was bedfast, so I thank God for even the pain. Although," he added honestly, "I'd probably be even more grateful for a back without pain."

Father Cooper smiled. "There is good in everything. Even my inconvenience today brought me a new friend, yes?"

"I don't know that I see good in all things," John said and there was a sadness in his voice. He thought of Joelle. "I don't see the original accident as being all that good."

"Tell me what happened."

John relayed some of the details of his crash, then added, "It was because of the crash that my family and fiancée were in Columbus when Pancho Villa and his men raided back in March. The woman I planned to marry was brutally attacked."

Father Cooper took on a new interest, eyeing John carefully. "Was she killed?"

"No," John said with a shake of his head. "She lived, but before I could recover from my own injuries, she ran away." John reached inside his pocket and pulled out Joelle's picture. "I'm searching for her and even though it's been months since I last saw her, I'll never stop until I find her." He handed the photograph to Father Cooper and went back to the task of eating.

Father Cooper stared at the dark eyes that stared back at him from the picture. It was just as he had come to suspect. Glancing from the picture to John, he was glad that the young man had not watched his reaction. He was equally glad that John did not ask if he had seen the young woman, for Father Cooper would never have lied about it.

Stunned to realize that John was the man Joelle so often spoke of, Father Cooper could only hand back the photograph in silence. There would be much praying to do, he thought silently, much praying, indeed.

## thirteen

Father Cooper was troubled and elated at the realization of who John really was. He knew that Joelle's future and happiness most probably lay in whether or not this young man's love for her was as strong as he seemed to believe it to be. After seeing John to a bed in the dormitory where he himself would sleep, Father Cooper began to pray about the matter and did not find his way into bed until late into the night.

John, relieved to feel even the marginal softness of the poorly stuffed mattress beneath him, had little difficulty falling asleep. It seemed one minute he was putting his head to the pillow and the next minute Father Cooper was standing over him, calling breakfast.

"I think I could probably sleep for a week straight," John sighed and kicked the covers away.

"Your body and mind are weary and you carry a great weight. It is not easy to be laden as you are. Come. Dress for breakfast and you can tell me more about your little friend. In case you are turned around, the water closet in which you bathed last night is at the end of the hall."

John dressed quickly, pulling on the same dusty jeans he had worn the day before. The pain in his back and legs was considerably lessened and despite still feeling tired, he was greatly improved. Finishing, he took a halfway clean shirt out from his bag and tried to tidy his appearance by wearing it. Then after a quick shave he joined Father Cooper in the dining room.

"Ah, you feel better, no?" Father Cooper smiled, pulling a chair out for John to use.

"I'm a new man," John smiled and limped to his chair.

John was surprised when two white clad Sisters appeared and placed food on the table before him. The aroma wafted up to greet him and John's stomach growled a hearty greeting.

"It sure smells good," he said and waited for Father Cooper to bless the meal.

They ate in silence for several minutes. John nearly inhaled the food before him and found that the Sisters were happy to refill the plate again when he had finished. Rolling scrambled eggs up inside a tortilla, John happily continued the feast.

"Please tell me about your young woman," Father Cooper suddenly encouraged and John's hand halted midway to his mouth.

With a sad smile, John spoke. "Her name is Joelle. We met in Bandelero. That's where I'm from." Father Cooper nodded and John continued. "She came to visit her brother once and I met her at a Christmas party. She was young and sweet, very naive and ever so popular with all the young men."

"But you won her heart, eh?" the priest grinned, causing the wrinkles on his face to shift.

John smiled. "Yes. It was almost love at first sight. At least, I was in love at first sight. I think Joelle was, too. She didn't seem to have nearly as much to say to anyone else and when I'd interrupt one of the other men's conversations, she always looked happy about it. One thing led to another and we started writing letters. I joined the army so I could fly planes. There wasn't but a handful of people doing it and I'm afraid I lied when I joined up and told them I was already a crack pilot."

"Your story did not catch up with you?"

"I was lucky," John replied. "No, I was destined to fly. I watched and listened, even read what little I could find on the matter. I finally managed to get taken under the wing of a good man, Bob Camstead. He saw through my story, but he also saw my drive. It wasn't long before we were working as a team. Later, when the army promoted him, we didn't get to fly together." John shrugged his shoulders. "But we stayed good friends."

"And what did the young woman think of your flying?"

"She loved it. I snuck her a ride once," John said and a light came into his eyes at the memory. "I went off without permission and flew one of the army planes home, just so I could see my sister, Angeline, get married to my best friend, Gavin Lucas. Before I left, Joelle was at my side, insisting I take her up. I think that's when I knew for sure that I could never love another woman as I loved her."

"But what of your love now? She has fled with her sorrow and you are here." Father Cooper seemed intent on an answer and John could not help but wonder what he should say.

"I only wish I knew. My love for her is as strong as ever. But, I don't know how she feels. She ran away after she was. . ." He could not say the word.

"Raped?"

"Yes. Such an ugly word and such a hideous thing," John muttered.

"She was unable to face you with her shame, is that so?"

"I guess," John replied softly. "I never saw it as her shame. She didn't do anything to deserve it. She was protecting my mother and me. I was still unable to walk when Villa attacked. They were killing soldiers and Joelle was certain they would kill me if they found me. She was probably right, but it doesn't make her sacrifice any easier to stomach."

"Why do you say that?"

"Because I feel like I let her down. I failed her because I couldn't keep her safe from harm. How can any woman go on trusting a man after that?"

"This woman sounds capable of a great many things."

"Oh, that she is," John agreed. "I just pray she's been able to put the attack behind her. I want to find her and take care of her."

"It will be difficult to put such a thing aside," Father Cooper said, putting down his fork. "Your accident is not yet behind you and you must deal with it constantly, no?" He did not wait for an answer but continued. "You did not choose to crash your airplane, but you did choose to fly. You knew the possibilities of crashing and yet you still chose to pursue that vocation."

"Yes," John said with a nod. The words could have very well been his own. "I told my mother that a pilot always lives with the knowledge that something can go wrong." He stopped for a minute. "Joelle came to care for me in Columbus. I didn't want her there. I didn't want her to see me helpless and beaten down. I made the choice to fly and the accident was my consequence to deal with, not hers. She never bargained for that kind of thing when she agreed to marry me."

"Ah, but neither then did you bargain to deal with this attack," Father Cooper declared.

"True, but Joelle didn't have a choice. I chose to fly. She didn't choose to be raped. She had no control, no say. She did what she did to unselfishly protect the people she loved."

Father Cooper toyed with a mug of now lukewarm coffee. He seemed to consider John's words quite profound. "It is well that you see this," he finally told John. "Your Joelle may struggle for a long time with the things that were done to her. As you said, her choices were taken from her. She was without the power to make that decision, beyond of course, the choice to protect you. However, an attack such as she must have endured is not a thing easily put aside. She may always suffer from it and never be capable of a physical closeness. Are you willing to give up such a thing?"

John felt startled by the priest's words. "I don't think I ever considered that. I mean, well, my father did mention the possibility."

"You may find your Joelle and also find that she is unable to return the love that you hold for her. Her scars may run so deep, that for a long, long time, she may be unwilling to love again."

John squared his shoulders and sat back in the chair. "Then I'll just wait her out."

Father Cooper smiled. "Your love can endure this wait?"

"If it has to." John knew that he spoke the truth. What was life without Joelle? Loving another woman was not even a consideration. "I'll wait as long as it takes. I know she's been hurt, but I believe my love for her will go far to heal her. She has to realize that the rape means nothing to me, at least as far as my love for her is concerned. I'll help her learn to put it in the past and forget about it. She won't need to carry it with her because I'll fill her heart and mind with the happiness and love that I know God has in store for us."

Father Cooper sobered again. "You forget there is the possibility that she may be unable to leave the attack in the past."

"I don't understand."

"There is always the chance that she suffered further consequences from the rape. She may be with child."

The words were like a slap in the face to John. His color paled considerably and he pushed back from the table with a startled expression. "I never thought of that." Getting up, he leaned against the chair and stared down at Father Cooper. "I never even considered that possibility."

"But it is one that you must consider. Especially before you go on and locate her. Should you find this situation is so, your rejection of her at that point could very well kill her." Father Cooper could picture Joelle's hurt expression in his mind. He would not risk her tenuous contentment by bringing to her a man who could never accept her fate.

John swallowed hard and looked away. *A child*, he thought. It was possible, just as Father Cooper said. He would always love Joelle, but could he love a child who had been forced upon her? A child conceived out of her most hated nightmare?

"I have to think," he said, suddenly breaking the silence. "I have to be alone." He grabbed up his cane and limped quickly from the room.

Father Cooper lifted his eyes heavenward. *Such pain and*

*suffering for children so young*, he thought. There was only one way to help them and that way was to pray.

॰

John walked back to his room and sat there in the silence for several minutes. In all of his dreams of finding Joelle, he had never once considered the chance that she could be pregnant. Why hadn't his father mentioned it when talking to John? He had certainly mentioned the fact that Joelle would probably fear physical intimacy. Daniel had talked at length with his son regarding the complications that might arise from Joelle's experience, but never once had he thought to mention a child.

Picking up his Bible, John knew that God would hold the only answers. Could he possibly look into the face of a baby born out of that rape and love it? The attack had cost him, as well as Joelle, although he knew her price to be much greater. Could she, herself, give birth to a child from that ordeal and nurture it at her breast. . .and call it her own?

"Oh, God," John whispered, "why must this happen? I don't even know if Joelle is with child, but if she is, how could it ever be a good thing?"

John's hand stopped roaming the pages of Scripture that he held and his eyes fell to the writing of Matthew 1:18-20.

"Now the birth of Jesus Christ was on this wise: When as his mother Mary was espoused to Joseph, before they came together, she was found with child of the Holy Ghost. Then Joseph her husband, being a just man, and not willing to make her a public example, was minded to put her away privily. But while he thought on these things, behold, the angel of the Lord appeared unto him in a dream saying, Joseph, thou son of David, fear not to take unto thee Mary thy wife: for that which is conceived in her is of the Holy Ghost."

John considered the words, lifted his eyes, and whispered, "But Mary's Child was Your Son and His conception was a glorious act of love."

John thought for a moment of how Joseph must have felt when he received the news of Mary's pregnancy. Did Joseph feel the anguish that John was feeling at this moment. Were there doubts and hesitations as to whether he could love Mary's Child?

"There must have been," John whispered. "Joseph must have been as troubled as I am or God would have had no need to send an angel to him."

The turmoil in John's heart began to lift. "I cannot compare the possible child who Joelle might be carrying, to Jesus, Father," John prayed, "but I am just a man, like Joseph, and my fears are deep in this matter. If there is a baby, what should I do?"

John knew the story of Joseph and Mary by heart. Christmas was a festive celebration of the birth of his Lord and always had been so as he had grown up. Some of his fondest memories surrounded the telling of this story of love between Mary and Joseph. He instantly recalled to mind a time when his Uncle David had preached on Joseph's faith.

"Joseph was just a carpenter. A simple man, who worked with his hands. He was probably considered a good man by his neighbors and friends. He no doubt kept the Commandments in the best way he knew how. He was certain to have appeared in the synagogue whenever it was appropriate to do so and he was betrothed to marry a girl.

"No doubt Joseph had his moments, just like the rest of us. He probably wondered if he was making enough money to support a wife and eventually a family. He probably felt concerned about the condition of his home and business. Maybe the roof leaked and he wondered how he was going to get everything fixed up before Mary came to live there." The congregation had smiled at this and John could not help but smile now as he remembered it.

"But," Uncle David's words continued to come back to John, "Joseph was to receive a bigger concern. Joseph was given a shock that must have come pretty hard to deal with. He was going to be a father. A father of a child he knew nothing about. A father of a child that was not his flesh and blood and had not come out of his doing."

John looked back at the Bible. If Joelle were expecting a child, it would be the same for him. He was engaged to marry Joelle and the child would not be of his doing.

"But Mary carried the Son of God," John said defensively. "Of course, Joseph could accept that. He wouldn't have to deal with wondering whose Child it was and Mary certainly didn't have to face the retribution. . ." John's words fell silent. Maybe he was wrong.

It was entirely possible that Mary had suffered just as Joelle might be, if she were expecting a child without a husband. Surely there were those who did not believe Mary's explanation. Even Joseph had to be convinced by an angel of God, before he found peace of heart in the matter.

"There must have been those who scoffed at them," John thought aloud sadly. He pictured the young couple who must have faced the doubtful faces of disbelievers. "But You would have protected them," John added thoughtfully. "You knew ahead of time how folks would react and You gave Your Son, even knowing that eventually people would kill Him. If You didn't spare Your Own Son, Jesus, from the persecution and ugliness of this world, how can I expect that You would keep it from me or Joelle?"

John's sudden revelation made him feel ashamed. "Forgive me, Father," he said with tears brimming his eyes. "Forgive me for the prideful selfishness of my thoughts. It would be no fault of the babe, should Joelle bring a child into this world. I love her, Father. I love my beloved Joelle and I can love any child she bears."

A peace washed over John like a flood and, with it, he washed away the bitterness of his past. How could he hold onto the regret and pain and embrace the future with the hope that God had planted in his heart?

*

Father Cooper was on his knees in prayer when John came into the room. He started to back out the door, but the priest looked up at him with such expectation in his eyes, that John froze in place. The unspoken question in Father Cooper's eyes prompted John to speak.

"I love her. It doesn't matter what's happened. I will always love her and I want her for my wife."

"And if there is a child?" Father Cooper questioned.

"It doesn't matter," John insisted.

"You can love this child and raise it for your own?"

"It will be my own," John said confidently. "Any child Joelle bears, will share my name and my love."

Father Cooper crossed himself and, with a smile, got slowly to his feet. "Then there is something we must talk about."

John looked quizzically at the priest and cocked his head to one side. "What is it?"

"Come." The old man put his arm around John's shoulder. "I must tell you news of our Joelle."

# fourteen

Joelle moved slowly under the growing weight of her child. In another month, she would deliver the baby. By her best estimations, Joelle figured the child was due around Christmas.

She finished tidying the tiny church and took herself to Father Cooper's quarters. He was due back today and Joelle was quite happy for this. She had missed the old man and his company. He had helped her through so many hardships and yet Joelle knew she could not expect him to be responsible for her future needs.

Seeing the low supply of mesquite wood, Joelle went outside to bring in an armful. She had steadily added to the stack throughout the summer months and even though November had been very warm during the day, nighttime cold required a fire.

She wiped sweat from her forehead and bent over to retrieve the gnarled sticks of mesquite. The baby kicked in protest and Joelle rubbed her hand lightly across her stomach. She was growing used to the idea of motherhood and although she still feared the outcome and their future, Joelle felt God had given her a love for the child.

She refused, however, to consider the matter further than the baby itself. She could not bring herself to wonder about its father or how she would provide for its care. She could not allow herself the memory of John's love and their planned marriage because it hurt too much to realize what she had lost.

Gathering the sticks, Joelle sighed deeply. So much would change when the baby arrived. She had to make plans and all her considerations led her in the way of leaving Father Cooper's little community.

*If I stay*, she reasoned to herself, *he will only feel obligated to provide for us and there is little enough for him. The people here are generous and would gladly help, but how fair is it for me to thrust my burdens upon them? No*, Joelle thought, *I must go. But where?*

She had given considerable thought to the matter. She knew the best choice was to contact her parents and go home. They would love her despite the child she carried and knowing her mother as she did, Joelle knew that the child would also be loved. Still, it was hard to face the idea. Once she went home, John would no doubt learn of her whereabouts and come to her.

"Oh, John," she whispered, straightening under the load of wood. She wondered where he was and if he had ever recovered from his injuries. Nightly, she prayed for him, but never did she allow herself to linger on his memory. It was simply more than she could bear.

"If I go home, can I keep you from coming to me?" she wondered aloud.

The day's heat continued and Joelle was exhausted from her tasks. She had replenished the wood supply, beaten the sand from all of the rugs, and seen to it that a pot of beans sat soaking on the stove. Should Father Cooper not return until tomorrow, Joelle reasoned that she would cook the beans for herself.

Taking off the scarf she had worn on her head, Joelle

dabbed at the sweat on her neck and brow. The aching in her back was fierce and she longed to rest. Perhaps a short nap was in line, she thought. Seeing that nothing else could be done for Father Cooper, Joelle took herself home and stretched out on her own bed.

Her furnishings were simple, even stark, especially in contrast to that which she had known growing up. She thought again of going home to her parents in Kansas City. Memories drifted through her mind of times spent in the huge house she had shared with her brothers and sister. She had had everything a child could want and, being the youngest, she had been spoiled beyond reason.

Clothes were her passion, she remembered with a smile. Her closets were overflowing with the latest fashions in an array of colors and materials. Now, she wore simple, peasant clothes and, running her hand down over the over-sized blouse, Joelle laughed out loud. Her friends would never recognize the woman she had become.

The thought of her friends brought to mind other things. She recalled dances and parties and games of lawn tennis. There was always something going on. She had enjoyed wealth and affluence, yet her parents had seen to it that her values were not placed in money and things. She had matured with the notion that money was only good so long as it was being used to benefit and not harm. Things could not buy peace of mind, Joelle knew. Just as money and things could not help her now.

She faded off to sleep thinking on these things, but the simple peace was again taken from her when images of the attack rose up to haunt her.

Joelle could smell the smoke and the foul stench of her attackers. It always started that way and it seemed as though it always would. She struggled to refuse the memories, but her mind was not willing to let the scene pass. Tossing and turning, fighting the attack in her sleep, Joelle opened her mouth to scream and felt strong arms encircle her.

Joelle slapped at the hands that sought her. She battled with their hold and tried to move away. She suddenly realized in sheer terror, that the hands that held her were not merely conjured in sleep, but were very real.

Her eyes snapped open in horror. The image before her was one of her attackers and she reached out with her hands to push away the man before her.

"Joelle, wake up. Joelle, it's me." John called to her over and over, knowing that she was lost in her nightmare.

Joelle heard the words, but it was the voice that caused her to still. She knew that voice. Squeezing her eyes closed, Joelle concentrated on the sound.

"Joelle, beloved." The voice sounded again.

"John," she whispered and opened her eyes to the vision of his face.

"Yes, it's me, Joelle," he said with a softness that melted away her fears.

Joelle allowed him to hold her for a moment as her mind struggled to comprehend his appearance.

John thought his heart would break at the look of fear in her eyes. Father Cooper had so kindly brought him to her, but when he had first laid eyes on her sleeping face, John knew the anguish of her attack was still a very real presence in her life.

He had watched her wrestle with her fears and when it seemed that the nightmare might best her, he could not resist pulling her into his arms. How could he have known that she would feel only more frightened by the action? He was still pondering this and wondering what he should do, when Joelle suddenly pushed him away.

"Get out of here, John. I don't know how you found me, but I want you to leave." The realization that he was here and that he knew her condition was more than Joelle could deal with.

John stared at her in confusion for a moment. "Joelle, don't be afraid. I've come to take you home. I've come to make you my wife."

Joelle shook her head and pushed at him with all of her strength. "Go away!" Her voice sounded strange to her. "Get out! I don't want you here! I don't want you to see me like this!"

"It's all right, Joelle. I love you."

She sobered for a moment. "I said the same to you once, after the accident. You told me to go away then and I'm telling you to leave now. You remember the pain. Don't be so cruel as to stay."

John reached out slowly to take her hand. "I remember."

Joelle felt his touch and tried to recoil. When he would not allow her to move from his grip, Joelle looked down at his hand as it lay against her swollen abdomen.

"We have to talk, Joelle. I've missed you so much and I've searched for you so very long. Don't try to make me go without even letting me tell you my heart."

Joelle felt her body begin to tremble. She was acutely aware of John's surprise when the baby kicked against their hands. Her eyes looked up to catch his expression of wonder.

"No," she said in a wavering voice. "You have to go."

"Joelle," the gentle voice of Father Cooper sounded from the doorway.

Looking up at the old man, Joelle was torn between a feeling of happiness at his return and betrayal for the man he had obviously brought with him. Her questioning gaze caused him to step forward.

"You should at least hear out what your young man has to say, no? He has journeyed far and suffered much for his love of you."

Joelle moved her glance from Father Cooper to John and back again. "He should have never come."

"But he did," the priest reminded. "The very least you can do is listen to him. He isn't here to harm you, Joelle. You know that as well as I do."

Joelle swallowed hard and tried to still her fears. "Very well. I will listen to him."

Father Cooper nodded. "I will be seeing to my flock."

He left the room as quietly as he had entered and Joelle returned her eyes to John. "You should have never come."

John grinned. "Just like you should have never come to Columbus when I crashed the Jenny."

"That was different."

John shook his head. "I didn't want you to be there, just as you don't want me here. Yet," he smiled even broader, "we both know I was just being stubborn and that I was really glad to see you. What of you, Joelle? Aren't you really glad to see me?"

"It doesn't matter," Joelle stated in a quiet, reserved manner.

"I believe it does."

"Well, I don't!" her voice sounded harsh. "If I'd wanted to see you, John, I would have come back to Bandelero."

John was undaunted. He had fully expected her anger. He let go of her hand and touched her stomach lightly. With a look of love in his eyes, he spoke. "I worked so hard to walk again," he began, "and all because I had to find you. When you disappeared, I thought I would die. I prayed and cried out to God to bring you back. I had J.D. looking all over El Paso for you. There isn't a law enforcement officer in this state, or Texas for that matter, who doesn't have a copy of your photograph."

Joelle's eyes widened in surprise, yet she said nothing. She was mesmerized by the gentleness of his voice. "I had to find you, Joelle. I love you so much. We are destined to spend our lives together, forever."

Joelle shook her head. "No, the raid changed all of that."

"Did the raid change your love for me?" His eyes pierced her façade of anger. She refused to answer him and looked away. Gently, John's hand took hold of her chin and drew her face back to his. "Did it? Did the attack you endured cause you to stop loving me?"

Joelle felt a tear slide down her cheek. There were no words for what she felt. How could she tell him that she still loved him? He would only feel more obligated.

John seemed to know what she was thinking. "Tell me that you no longer love me and I'll go. Tell me the raid caused your love for me to die and I'll never force you to lay eyes on me again."

"No," Joelle sobbed and struggled to regain control. "My love didn't die."

"And neither did mine."

"But I can't hold you to that," Joelle protested. "I released you from our engagement. I'd hoped you would find happiness elsewhere, with someone worthy of your love."

"Ah, Joelle," he murmured her name and it sounded like a song. "You are more than worthy. I'm the one who acted badly. I tried to push you away when you knew I needed you most and now," he paused and slowly smiled, "you're trying to do the same. It won't work, you know."

"I can't hold onto the past," Joelle stated flatly. "You

have no obligation here. I broke our engagement when I left Columbus."

"Well, I didn't accept the break," John countered. "I don't release you, Joelle."

"Go home, John. Just put me from your mind and go home." Her voice was weary. "I can't bear the sorrow of seeing you here."

"You are a coward, Joelle Dawson, but I love you, all the same." He used her own words from long ago, against her. Joelle kept shaking her head as he continued. "I don't release you from your obligation to marry me and until you're able to do something about it, I consider myself your husband-to-be." John grinned. "You're stuck with me, just as I was stuck with you then."

Joelle pushed him away. "You can't be expected to stay with me now."

"And why not? My love was never conditional."

"You didn't ask for this," she shouted with a wave of her hand over her protruding stomach.

"And neither did you." John said firmly. "Funny, but this conversation sounds mighty familiar."

"It's not the same, John, so don't try to make it that way!"

John got to his feet. "It is the same and you really are a coward."

"How dare you!" Joelle moved from the bed as gracefully as her size would allow. "How dare you!"

"I dare because it's true. You're afraid and it's gotten the best of you. Surely it's much easier to live behind the wall of fear you've built for yourself, but I wonder," John said with a knowing look, "how long before the wall comes tumbling down and you have to face the truth of what's real?"

# fifteen

Joelle picked up the first object she could reach and hurled it across the room. John ducked with a grin, narrowly missing the empty glass as it shattered against the wall.

"At least you drank whatever was in it first," he commented, reminding Joelle of the scene she had exchanged with him. "Suppose we ought to lay in a supply of drinking glasses?"

Joelle's eyes blazed. "You can mock me all you want, John Monroe, and it isn't going to change a thing! I want you out of here! Go home and stop feeling sorry for me."

John crossed his arms against his chest and blocked the door with his body. "I'm not going anywhere and neither are you. At least not until we get this talked out."

"I'm in no mood to talk to you about anything." Joelle mimicked John's action by crossing her arms. For a moment they faced off without words.

"Joelle," John whispered her name. "Marry me."

Joelle's anger surged again. "No! I won't ever marry anyone. I'm not worthy of anyone. Don't you understand? The attack changed all of that!"

"It changed nothing."

Joelle stormed at him with her hands raised. "It changed everything! Are you blind? I'm carrying another man's child. I don't even know which man's child. There were three of them, you know!"

John reached out to still her flailing arms. "No, I didn't know that. I didn't know because you shut me out and ran away. I'm sorry, Joelle, but it still doesn't change my love for you."

"It can't be the same!" she screamed, fighting against his hold.

"Of course not," John reasoned softly. "No one said it would be. I don't even want it to be the same. I was so selfish and lost in myself back then. I surely wouldn't want you to have to live with that man." John pulled her tighter to him and the baby clearly took issue with the action.

"This baby will always be between us," Joelle protested and tears began to fall.

"No," John whispered, "this baby will always be a part of us."

Joelle began to sob in earnest. She stopped fighting John's hold and buried her face against his shoulder. "I don't know who the father is."

"I'm the father," John declared. "I'm the only father this child will ever have. . .the only one he'll ever need."

She had no idea how long she let him hold her. She only knew that the comfort he offered was exactly what she had longed for. It dispelled her fears that John's touch would be just like that of her attackers. She had worried she might never again be able to feel the embrace of a man without being reminded of the rape. But this embrace reminded her only of the love she had known with John. This embrace gave her hope.

Silently, John led her back to the bed and pulled her down to sit on the side of it with him. Joelle raised her head and caught sight of the broken glass on the floor. It seemed to stun her momentarily.

"I don't know why I did that," she said, surprising them both.

John smoothed back her hair. "You did it because you were angry and helpless."

"Yes," Joelle nodded, "I am angry."

John put a finger under her chin and lifted her face to his. "Anger is normal, Joelle. After all you've been through, you are quite entitled to your anger. It's what you do with that anger that makes a difference. The Bible even says we can get angry, but we aren't to sin out of that anger."

"I don't understand," Joelle said wearily.

"But God does, Joelle." John's eyes were soft and warm. "We can get through this with His help. It's time to move ahead."

"I don't know if I can."

"You have to," John said with a smile. "You have no choice. You're going to have baby. A baby who's going to need you and need your love."

"John," she whispered his name, "I'm not the girl you fell in love with. I'll never be whole again. There will always be a part of me that's damaged and crippled."

John dropped his hold and got to his feet. "Then we'll be a perfect match."

"I don't understand. You aren't making any sense," Joelle said with a look of confusion.

John crossed the room to retrieve the cane he had left by the door. For the first time, Joelle noticed his limp. He turned back to her with a shrug of his shoulders. "Dad says I may never walk normal again. I might always need this cane. Do you love me less because of it?" He was completely serious and his expression betrayed a pain that mirrored Joelle's own.

"Of course not," she stated firmly. "But that's different."

"Why?" John asked her, coming back to the bed. "Why is it different?" Joelle could not answer and so he continued. "I struggle to forgive myself for letting you face those men alone. I wanted only to protect you and keep you safe from harm and it was because of me that you had to face the attack. It eats me up inside and I know it's something I'll always live with."

"I made my choice, John. I told you. . ." Her words fell silent as she remembered what she had said.

"You told me what?" John encouraged her to answer.

Joelle swallowed hard, dropping her gaze to the floor. "I told you anything was preferable to your death."

"And now you want to take that back, eh?"

"No!" she exclaimed, her head snapping up. "Never! You were unable to walk. They would have killed you. What happened wasn't your fault so there's no reason to blame yourself."

"It wasn't your fault, either, Joelle. The entire matter was taken out of your hands. I guess we both need to forgive ourselves." John picked up her hand and kissed her fingertips. "We have to forgive and let go of the past. We have to forgive ourselves and," he paused to take a tighter hold on her hand, "we have to forgive those men, as well."

"They don't deserve to be forgiven," she said flatly.

"Neither do we, but God extended us that privilege."

"But they deserve it even less. We aren't like them. Our sins aren't like theirs," Joelle protested.

"Isn't that up to God to judge?"

"I don't know."

"Yes, you do," John softly insisted. "You know as well as I do that no matter how undeserving those men are forgiving them is the only way we can go on and build a future. It's the only way we can leave them behind and concentrate on us.

"God offered us His Son, Jesus, as a means to receive forgiveness and salvation. We've both known the truth of that since we were children. And, if I remember correctly, we both made decisions to take Him up on that offer. Seems to me, just when trials came to us both, we questioned whether or not God was really and truly Who He said He was. That's human weakness and a lack of faith, but even that, God understands. We made a commitment to God. We accepted His free gift of salvation through Jesus. We repented of our sins and pledged to forgive others. Now, here we are, presented with that very situation, and you want to throw it all away?"

"No!" Joelle declared. "I don't want to do anything of the sort. I know God wants me to forgive." Joelle stopped. It was true. God had made it quite clear to her that forgiveness was the only way she could set herself free. Just like His forgiveness had set her free from eternal death.

"Your anger is a poor companion, Joelle. You have to break away from your old nature and let Jesus fill you with the new nature that only He can provide. I had to do it. I had to seek out God and His forgiveness. I had to admit that I was wrong and that even though He'd been faithful to me a million times before, when I came face to face with a monumental problem, I was still too human to trust. Our adversities can weaken us greatly, but He can make us strong despite their effects." John paused, seeing the conflict Joelle felt, mirrored in her eyes. "Forgive them, Joelle. Forgive them for their cruelty and let go of the anger that holds you captive."

Joelle felt a rush of emotion at the suggestion. She had lived so long with the nightmares that her anger seemed the only way to deal with her fear.

"I need to be alone. Please," she said with a pleading in her voice, "just let me think for a while."

John released her hand and got to his feet. "I guess that's reasonable enough. I'll be with Father Cooper if you need me." He went to the door without protesting, surprising himself as well as Joelle.

He turned back to look at her. She seemed so frail and small. It was his utmost desire to protect her and keep her safe from the pain and suffering she had known.

"Rise up, my love, my fair one, and come away. For, lo, the winter is past, the rain is over and gone." His eyes betrayed tears. His voice was a husky whisper as he added, "Come away, my love."

He spoke the words and then was gone, leaving Joelle to stare at the empty space where he had stood.

≈

Walking away was the hardest thing John had ever done. Now that he had found Joelle, all he wanted to do was cling to her. He certainly did not want to let her from his sight.

"Dear God," he prayed, "please give her the strength to get through this. Give her the strength to let go of her anger and fear. I love her so much."

He sat down on a chair, mindful of the pain in his back. He would carry that pain for a long time, just as Joelle would carry hers. Even in forgiveness, John realized, only time and healing would ease the pain.

Father Cooper's slight form passed by the window and John got to his feet and went outside to join him.

"All is well?" the priest asked, unable to read John's expression.

"I'm not sure," John replied. He leaned heavily against the cane.

"You must trust God, my son. He knows full well the sorrows you share with Joelle. He has brought you here for a purpose. The answers you've searched for are soon to be given. Trust Him to give you the strength to bear them."

"I just want her to be healed. I just want her to recover from the pain."

"Even if you cannot be a part of that recovery?" Father Cooper's words hit John hard.

A life without Joelle? How could he even imagine the possibility? "I don't want to live without her. I can't even bear the thought of it," John admitted.

"But, if that is required of you, are you willing to put aside your own desires for the betterment of Joelle?"

John realized he would do whatever it took to help Joelle. Even if he had to walk away from her forever, he knew he would do whatever was best for her. "If God shows me no other way," John said softly, "I'll leave."

"Your love for her is good, John," Father Cooper said, putting a supportive arm around his shoulders. "Come, let's give God time to speak to her heart."

❧

Joelle sat, silently staring at the four walls of her bedroom. She had called this place home for quite a while and yet it held no fond memories or happiness for her. It was a prison . . .a tomb, she thought. She had come here to live out her sentence and, in some ways, to die.

John's sweet face came to mind. Why had he come? How

did he find her? The questions raced through her head and yet Joelle knew the answers were unimportant. She thought back to the day she had first seen him after the accident. He was angry at God and everyone else, but mostly he was angry with himself.

"Just as I'm angry with myself," Joelle murmured. She smiled as she recalled the determination with which she had faced John during the early period of his confinement. "He won't back down," she realized aloud. "He's just like me when it comes to being stubborn."

Exhausted from her physical exertion, Joelle fell back against the pillows. She stared up at the ceiling and in that instant it triggered the memory of her rape. She remembered staring at the ceiling, fixing her eyes on a single spot, in order to keep from seeing the faces of the men who were hurting her.

Her breathing quickened. She could nearly feel their hands upon her. *Dear God*, she thought, *must I forever live with this*?

*Forgive them and leave them behind.* Wasn't that what John had spoken of not moments ago? *Forgive them?*

"They don't deserve to be forgiven," Joelle said with clenched fists and hot tears. "I want them to suffer, just as I have. I want them to know the same misery I've known."

*Give them to Me, Joelle.* The silent voice stirred her soul.

"No," she argued, "I can't. They took so much from me. They took everything."

*Give them to Me and I will give you rest.*

Joelle let go a sob. She was so tired, so very weary. The burden had been so great and the exhaustion from carrying it so complete.

"I want rest," she whispered. "I do want rest."

## sixteen

It was dark when Joelle awoke. She had slept peacefully in spite of her surprise at seeing John. A tapping sounded at her door and, sitting up with a yawn, Joelle called out.

"Come in." The soft glow of lamplight flooded the room. She expected to see John, but was taken back when, instead, Father Cooper poked his head inside the doorway.

"Are you feeling up to a talk?" he asked.

"Of course," she replied and awkwardly pushed up into a sitting position.

Father Cooper came in and placed the lamp beside her bed. "I hope you don't mind the imposition but I felt there are things between us that needed to be said."

"Things between us?" Joelle questioned with a puzzled expression.

Father Cooper drew up a chair and folded his hands. "I brought John with me from Las Cruces."

"So that's how he found me."

"Yes. It was actually God's doing, though." He paused and smiled in his way. "I had trouble with the touring car. It became stuck in the sand. John came riding up and freed me. We shared supper together and he told me of his mission to find you."

"I see," Joelle replied softly. "That must have come as quite a shock to both of you."

"John didn't know at first. I decided not to share my good

153

news with him until I was certain of his commitment to you. You see, Joelle," he paused, "I would never have allowed him to hurt you. I waited until I was assured of his sincere love for you before I shared your location with him."

Joelle shook her head. "But how could you be certain of his love? John's the type of person who upon hearing of my plight would instantly feel obligated to care for me."

"But I did not tell him of your circumstances, child. I did not reveal to him any knowledge of you whatsoever. I let John tell me about his search and about his love." Joelle started to speak but Father Cooper held up his hand. "Please, hear me out." Joelle nodded and waited for him to continue.

"I could see the anguish and misery in this young man. He was so filled with the longing to find you. He had already searched far and the very fact that he was on his feet was, in part, due to his determination to see you again."

"I can imagine that's true," Joelle stated, forgetting herself.

Father Cooper smiled. "I talked to John without letting him know I knew of you. I told him it was possible that the woman he loved would be forever scarred by what had happened in Columbus. You had said as much, yes?"

"Yes."

"I asked him if he could live with those scars and he assured me that what had happened to you had no bearing on his love for you. I believed him then, Joelle. I still believe him."

"But, Father Cooper, he couldn't possibly have known about the baby. Not unless you told him. Even so, he wouldn't have told you then that he couldn't marry me. John's not that type of person. He takes his obligations quite seriously."

"I did not tell him your were with child. At least not until after he assured me that such a thing would still be unimportant in respect to your future and his love."

"How did he convince you of this?"

"I merely suggested that a fear of physical intimacy was not the only possible residual effect of the rape. I asked him what he would do if he found you and then learned that you were with child."

Joelle paled a bit. "And what did he say?"

"It was something he'd not thought about. He left me for a time and came back with his answer, which was that he would love you and any child you bore. It changed nothing, Joelle. He still desired to find you and to make you his wife."

Joelle's eyes filled with tears. "He is a good man."

"Yes, that is definitely so."

"You once told me that even though we prayed in different ways and in different places, we still served the same God," Joelle said as she reached out her hand to the wizened priest. "I also believe that is so. You have taught me much about God and His love. You've showed me a side to God that I might never have seen. I can't say I am thankful for the attack or that I ask blessings for my attackers. However, I do believe I am ready to forgive and desperately ready to forget."

"It is well with your soul, eh?" Father Cooper questioned with a smile lighting up his eyes. "Our God is big enough for even these things that seem overwhelming."

"He seemed to have planned everything out in detail," Joelle replied. "Look at the way He put you and John together. Better yet, the way He put you and me together. He saw to my needs when I didn't even know what they were."

"He is like that, our God."

"Yes, He is."

"I am glad for you, Joelle. My heart sings within me and I know that God will bless you forever. If I can ever do anything more, please remember your old friend."

Joelle reached out and embraced the priest in a fierce hug. "I do love you, Father Cooper. You have given me so much."

"And you, also, have blessed me."

Joelle pulled back and wiped at her tears. "Would you consider one more favor?"

"What is it?"

"Would you marry John and me?"

The old man's face broke into a beaming smile. "I would love nothing more." He paused for a moment with a seriousness overtaking his joy. "But, you know you are not of my church and. . ."

"John and I will remarry in our church at home. His uncle is our pastor. I'd just like the memory of standing before you and God."

"Then we will treat it that way," Father Cooper said with a nod. "But, should you not find your young man and let him know your heart? He was quite worried when last we spoke."

Joelle nodded. "Where is he?"

"He was walking down by the river."

Joelle got to her feet and, reaching to the end of her bed, she took up the warm, hand-woven blanket that lay there. "I will be walking by the river, Father Cooper," she said, pulling the blanket around her shoulders.

≈

John lingered by the water's edge long after the sun had set. He was so unsure of how Joelle would respond to his coming. He had prayed and sought peace and knew in his heart that if he had to leave her, he would. But he would never again be whole. . .not without her love.

Sitting there on the river bank, John silently thought of his life in Bandelero. What would he do when he returned? He had spent so much time just trying to heal. If Joelle did agree to come home and be his wife, how would he ever support them?

"Are you brooding or dreaming?" Joelle's soft voice called out from behind him.

Getting slowly to his feet, John limped to where she stood. "Both," he confessed. In the moonlight he could see her smile.

She glanced down at the hand in which John held his cane. She put her own hand atop his and looked up into his eyes. "We should talk."

"Yes."

"Would you like to sit again?" Joelle asked, mindful of his condition.

"Would you?"

"Yes, I believe so," she replied, patting her stomach. "It becomes increasingly more difficult to get around. You'll have to help me."

John reached out and took her by the elbow. "I've got the perfect place for us." He led her to the river bank and helped her to sit. Joining her there, he found himself nearly holding his breath. "You wanted to talk?"

"Yes," Joelle said and took a deep breath. "You were right to come. I'm glad you came." She paused for a moment to look out into the darkness. "It's impossible to know what's out there," she said absently.

John thought it profound. "Yes, but what we have here is

easy to see."

Joelle turned and smiled. "We won't have it easy elsewhere."

"Probably not."

"We will start life at a great disadvantage," she murmured.

"We'll have each other."

"And a child," Joelle reminded.

"Yes. A beautiful child, born of a lovely and beautiful woman," John whispered, running a finger along Joelle's cheek.

Joelle's breath caught at the pleasure his actions caused. She stared longingly into his eyes for several moments, waiting and hoping that he might kiss her. *Kiss me*, she thought. *I have to know it's all that it once was.* When John refused to initiate the action, Joelle leaned forward and put her hand up to his face.

"Please, kiss me," she whispered in the silence of the night.

John's eyes took on a fire that she had once known long ago. He leaned closer to meet her lips and put his hand gently behind her head. The kiss was sweet and heartfelt and everything that Joelle had hoped it would be. She found herself clinging to John with such joy flooding her heart that she could scarcely believe it was real.

He pulled away first, leaving Joelle with a smile on her lips. Her eyes were still closed as she relished the moment.

"I remember the first time you kissed me," Joelle whispered and slowly opened her eyes. "Do you?"

"How could I forget? It was under the mistletoe at Maggie and Garrett Lucas's Christmas party. It was the moment I decided to marry you."

She grinned. "You'd just met me. How could you have decided a thing like that?"

"It was easy. I knew what I was looking for."

Joelle frowned ever so slightly. "A lot has happened since then, John. Are you sure I'm still what you're looking for?"

"More than ever," he replied, his voice hoarse with emotion. "I love you, Joelle. Now and for all time."

"No matter the past?"

"No matter the past, the present, or the future." John pulled her close. "My love for you will only grow stronger. You are my beloved."

" 'I am my beloved's, and my beloved is mine,' " she quoted from the sixth chapter of the Song of Solomon. A warmth spread throughout her body. "I am yours, John, if you still want me."

"Can there be any doubt?" he said and lifted her face to meet his kiss. Joelle melted against him and was sorry when he pulled away.

"Well," she said with a sigh, "if there were any doubts, I believe you've dispelled them all. You are one stubborn man, John Monroe."

He laughed heartily. "No more so than you, Joelle Dawson."

"We'll probably fight," she said quite seriously.

"Yes, very probably."

"Will you throw mugs?" she asked with a grin.

"Only if you throw drinking glasses."

"You were right about me being a coward," she said thoughtfully.

"Ummm," John sounded with a glance upward, "I hate to admit it, but you were right about me being a coward, as well."

"You? Never!" she exclaimed.

"It's true," John replied. "I was afraid in Columbus. I was afraid I would be bedfast forever and never know what it was like to walk beside you again. I was afraid in Columbus, when you left me and ran away. I was afraid when I couldn't find you and my search seemed in vain." He stopped and looked deep into her velvety eyes. "And then when I did find you, I was afraid that you'd stopped loving me."

Joelle put her finger to his lips. "That, I could never do, so put it from your mind and don't be afraid any longer."

"What of you, Joelle? Are you still afraid?"

She dropped her hand and looked away. "I'm terrified."

"Of me?"

"No," she whispered and drew his hand to her stomach. "This."

John placed his arm around her shoulder. "Don't be. I'll be with you every step of the way. Babies are wondrous things and I hope we have a dozen."

Joelle's head came up in surprise. "A dozen? I thought four sounded like a nice number."

John smiled. "Whatever you say."

"You realize, of course," she said with a sudden thought, "this particular child is due next month."

"That soon, huh? I guess we'd better think about getting home then so Dad can deliver it."

Joelle nodded. "That would probably be wise."

"We probably ought to think about something else, as well," John said without reserve. "Don't you suppose we ought to get married?"

"I'm way ahead of you on that one, Mr. Monroe. Father

Cooper is waiting, even now, to perform a lovely ceremony for us. I thought it might be nice for him to be a part of our marriage, since he's partially responsible for bringing us together again. After we get home, your Uncle David could marry us, if that meets with your approval."

"I see you have this all under control," John grinned.

"Do you mind?"

"Not in the least. I think it sounds wonderful. Come on," he said, getting to his feet. "I want to get married."

## seventeen

"John!" Joelle screamed out his name in the agonizing final stages of labor.

"What!" John yelled from outside the room where his wife was giving birth.

"I've changed my mind!"

Dan and Lillie exchanged a look of amusement with Joelle's mother. John and Joelle had been yelling back and forth at each other for hours now and neither one seemed to think the exchange unusual.

"It's a little late for that, darling!" John called back.

Joelle grimaced as another contraction gripped her. She waited for it to pass before explaining her thoughts. "Not about having this baby," she yelled. "I've changed it about having four of them!"

Zandy and Lillie laughed out loud, while Daniel tried to concentrate on the task at hand. There was an amused smile on his lips, however.

"Whatever you say, dear!" John yelled back and grinned at his father-in-law. "I love that woman."

Riley shook his head and laughed. "She's not your run-of-the-mill society girl, is she?"

"Thank God for that," John mused with a laugh. He grew sober however, when Joelle's scream filled the air. "How much longer do you suppose this will go on?"

Riley shrugged. "It always seems like forever." John

nodded and resumed his pacing.

Inside their bedroom, Joelle bore down with all her might to expel the child from her body. "Mother!" she gasped and gripped Zandy's hand tightly. "I want this to be over with."

"It will, darling, just a little longer. You'll see." Zandy wiped her daughter's brow with a cool cloth and prayed for the delivery to be an easy one.

Joelle rolled her head from side to side. She was suddenly overcome with fear. "Mother, what if the baby is hideous? What if it looks like one of them?" Joelle had tried to force such thoughts from her mind these last few weeks, but the old fears caught up with her.

Zandy soothed her daughter with words of encouragement. "Joelle, no baby is hideous. Your child will be beautiful and precious. You'll see." She prayed silently for her daughter, knowing that only God could give her peace in the matter.

"That's right, Joelle," Lillie assured her. "Once you see the baby, all your fears will disappear.

"And from the looks of it, that's going to be in just another minute or two," Dan said confidently.

Joelle felt the contractions begin again. They were coming one after the other now. The urge to bear down and push was stronger than ever. "I...don't...want," she gasped against the pain.

"Don't want what, sweetheart?" her mother asked softly.

"Let...John...see...first!"

"See what, Joelle?" Zandy questioned.

"The baby!" Joelle said and screamed out in pain. "Let...him...see the baby...first."

"Push, Joelle," Dan commanded. "Push hard."

Joelle bore down with all her might. She was exhausted from the entire ordeal. "John!" she screamed and was answered with the sound of a baby's cry.

"It's a girl, Joelle!" Lillie announced, as Dan passed the squalling child over. "We have a granddaughter, Dr. Monroe."

Joelle fell back against the pillow and threw her arm across her face. "Mother, pray with me. Please."

Zandy leaned her lips down to Joelle's ear. The baby continued to cry while Lillie cleaned her up.

"Please, God," Zandy whispered in prayer, "please strengthen Joelle and help her through this frightening time in her life. Give her peace of mind and a love for her daughter that will surpass her fear, Amen."

Joelle pulled her arm away to look into her mother's face. There were tears in her eyes. "Where's John? Please let John come in."

Zandy looked at Dan, who nodded his approval. She went quickly to the door and motioned for her son-in-law to join them. In a hushed voice she told him of Joelle's request.

"She's afraid to see the baby. She wants you to see her first."

John nodded a look that held no condemnation. He knew of Joelle's fears and he could not fault her for them. Stepping to where Lillie was now wrapping the baby in a warm blanket, he could only stare in wonder.

"You have a daughter," Lillie said, handing to her first-born child, his own firstborn. "Now this is what I call some Christmas present."

John looked down at the tiny bundle. The baby calmed

in his arms and stared back at him with dark, wet eyes. She was beautiful! The most beautiful thing he had ever seen in his life, with the possible exception of Joelle. He smiled broadly at his mother and Zandy.

"She's perfect," he said with assurance.

"She looks like Joelle did," Zandy said and there was no stopping the flow of tears from her eyes. "I have to go tell Riley," she said and took herself from the room.

Dan finished his tasks and patted Joelle on the hand. "You did a great job, Mommy. I think this is the best Christmas present I've ever had. Not everybody gets a granddaughter in their stocking." Joelle tried to smile, but her teeth began to chatter. "Lillie, do we have another blanket?" Dan asked.

Lillie nodded and left John to fuss over his daughter. She pulled a huge quilt from the drawer beneath the bed and unfolded it to cover Joelle. "I always got the shivers after delivery," she grinned down. "This ought to warm you right up."

"Thanks," Joelle whispered, relishing the feel of the added weight.

"Come on, Grandma," Dan said with a laugh. "Let's call up the town and announce our new granddaughter!" Lillie nodded and linked her arm with Dan's. They exited the room to join the laughter and conversation of Riley and Zandy, thoughtfully closing the door behind them.

John looked up from the baby to catch Joelle's worried look. "She's precious, Joelle. She has your coloring and your eyes. She has your cute little mouth and she can yell almost as loud."

Joelle could not help but smile. "Does she have any hair?"

"A ton of it and it's all dark brown like her mom's."

Joelle bit at her lower lip as the baby started to fuss. "Bring her to me," she finally said and John quickly complied before she could change her mind.

He lowered the baby into Joelle's arms, while Joelle kept her eyes on John's face. Joelle felt the warm softness of the infant and the natural way she seemed to fit against her. The baby calmed.

John kissed Joelle on the forehead. "She's perfect. Just look at her."

For only a moment, Joelle thought back to Columbus. Then pushing the image aside, she lowered her face to the bundle in her arms.

Two dark eyes stared up at her with a sweet, tiny mouth opened wide in a yawn. Joelle felt a surge of relief and tears came to her eyes. "Oh, John," she whispered. She reached up her finger to touch the velvety softness of the baby's cheek.

"I told you she was perfect," he said with a smile.

"Oh, she truly is," Joelle murmured. "How could I have feared this?"

"No doubt she'll give our poor hearts plenty to fear in the future. The first time she climbs a tree or runs away from home."

"She'd better never!" Joelle declared.

"Well, if she's anything like you, she no doubt will," John insisted.

"Well, if she takes after you, she'll probably be hanging out of the cockpit of a biplane and soaring overhead."

John smiled at Joelle's reference. "No daughter of mine will hang out of the cockpit of a biplane," he retorted indignantly.

"Oh, really?" Joelle laughed. "And who will stop her?"

"I will. If she can't sit in it properly and fly the thing professionally, then she won't be allowed to do it at all."

Joelle nodded. "With her daddy to teach her, she'll be a crackerjack pilot."

The baby yawned again and closed her eyes. John reached up and smoothed back Joelle's hair. "You've done a good thing here, Mrs. Monroe."

"Yes," Joelle said smugly and glanced up into his eyes. "I have, haven't I?" John raised a quizzical brow and Joelle laughed. "Of course," she added, "you and God had something to do with it, too. I couldn't have done it without your support and love, nor His."

"God has done something quite wondrous, hasn't He?"

"Indeed," Joelle agreed. "She's everything a mother could hope for. She's absolutely complete and perfect."

"Except for one thing," John said. "What shall we call her?"

"Oh, I was so busy worrying about the outcome, I never thought to plan a name for her."

"Well, let's see. It is Christmas. We could call her Christina."

"No," Joelle said shaking her head. "I like Holly."

"Hey, how about Mistletoe?" John teased. "After all, that's where we first kissed."

"I like Holly," Joelle repeated firmly.

"You sure?"

"Yes." Joelle nodded and ran her hand lightly over her daughter's tiny head. "Holly Noelle."

"Hey, it rhymes with Joelle. Sounds good to me." He planted a kiss on Joelle's forehead, then leaned over to do the same for the baby.

"Holly Noelle Monroe," Joelle breathed the name.

"I still think Mistletoe would have worked. We could've called her Missy," John said with a prankish smile.

Joelle rolled her eyes. "Her name is Holly."

"Well, maybe next time."

"Next time? I told you I'd changed my mind."

John nodded. "I thought you meant about having four. I just naturally presumed that meant we were going to try for twelve."

Joelle gave his ribs a hard nudge of her elbow, disturbing the baby's slumber as she did. Holly protested with a whimper, but quickly settled back to sleep.

"All right," John conceded. "You don't have to have any more, if you really don't want to."

Joelle was already forgetting about the pain of delivery. "Well, I'd hate for her to grow up an only child. I guess we'll see."

Outside, it had begun to snow and Joelle could see the light, downy flakes from where she lay. "Look," she whispered to John, "it's so lovely."

"No more so than you, beloved," John answered with a proud look of love in his eyes.

Joelle felt secure and happy in that look. "It truly will be all right, won't it, John? We're a family now and God can help us to rise above the hurt we've known. We'll make a good home for Holly."

"The best," John promised. "The very best God has to offer."

# epilogue

Panch Villa's raid on Columbus, New Mexico was a failure in that few Americans were killed and most of the money and valuables that were stolen were lost in the frantic retreat of the *Villistas*.

The most poignant effect of the raid was psychological. It caused panic throughout the border region of the U.S. and proved to the U.S. government that the Carrancista government could do nothing, or was unwilling to control Villa. It also made Americans aware that even in their neutral attitudes regarding the war in Europe, they were far from safe in the isolated cocoon they had woven for themselves.

Across America, many were opposed to the U.S. government's recognition and support of the *Carrancistas*, feeling that they were as bad, if not worse than the *Villistas*.

General Pershing's troops never managed to capture the elusive Pancho Villa. As the United States Army invaded deeper and deeper into Mexico, hostilities grew between the two countries and Villa became somewhat of a hero to his people. President Wilson found himself up against Carranza's rejection of U.S. interference in Mexican affairs, and even though Villa had attacked U.S. soil, Carranza wanted Pershing's troops immediately recalled.

Large amounts of money, along with the sweat and toil of the U.S. Army, were spent on the effort without success and the "Punitive Expedition" was rapidly deemed a failure.

By 1917, America headed into another four years with Wilson at the helm and Pershing still struggling to overtake Villa. The underlying hope of Germany at this point was to keep the Americans so completely engrossed in the border conflicts that they would be forced to stay on the opposite side of the Atlantic and leave them to their war conquests in Europe.

This might well have worked had it not been for the Zimmermann Telegram, in which Germany offered Mexico a military alliance in return for their declaration of war against the United States. The interception of this coded message made it clear to Wilson that our entry into what was to be called World War I was imminent. Our passive neutrality was broken and America went to war.

# A Letter To Our Readers

Dear Reader:

In order that we might better contribute to your reading enjoyment, we would appreciate your taking a few minutes to respond to the following questions. When completed, please return to the following:

Rebecca Germany, Managing Editor
Heartsong Presents
P.O. Box 719
Uhrichsville, Ohio 44683

1. Did you enjoy reading *Come Away, My Love*?
   ❏ Very much. I would like to see more books
      by this author!
   ❏ Moderately
      I would have enjoyed it more if _____

   _____

2. Are you a member of **Heartsong Presents**? ❏Yes ❏No
   If no, where did you purchase this book? _____

   _____

3. What influenced your decision to purchase this
   book? (Check those that apply.)

   ❏ Cover          ❏ Back cover copy

   ❏ Title          ❏ Friends

   ❏ Publicity      ❏ Other_____

4. How would you rate, on a scale from 1 (poor) to 5
   (superior), the cover design? _____

5. On a scale from 1 (poor) to 10 (superior), please rate the following elements.

    ___ Heroine    ___ Plot

    ___ Hero    ___ Inspirational theme

    ___ Setting    ___ Secondary characters

6. What settings would you like to see covered in **Heartsong Presents** books? _____

_____

_____

7. What are some inspirational themes you would like to see treated in future books? _____

_____

_____

8. Would you be interested in reading other **Heartsong Presents** titles? ❑ Yes    ❑ No

9. Please check your age range:
  ❑ Under 18    ❑ 18-24    ❑ 25-34
  ❑ 35-45    ❑ 46-55    ❑ Over 55

10. How many hours per week do you read? _____

Name _____

Occupation _____

Address _____

City_____ State_____ Zip _____

# *Christmas* **Treasures**

### *Four new love stories*
### *from Christmases past and present*

*An Ozark Christmas Angel* by **Veda Boyd Jones**
A sneaky matchmaker thinks Christmas would be
the perfect time for Lindsay and a certain doctor to fall in love.

*Christmas Dream* by **Tracie J. Peterson**
An Alaskan snowstorm grounds newlyweds Mark and Rita
Williams in the Juneau airport for their first Christmas together.

*Winterlude* by **Colleen L. Reece**
A single out-of-place snowflake in San Diego
lures Ariel Dixon to Ketchikan, Alaska,
home to a handsome childhood friend presumed dead.

*Dakota Destiny* by **Lauraine Snelling**
Two years after Mary received word
that Will is presumed dead in World War I,
she wants only to dream of his return.

(352 pages, Paperbound, 5" x 8")

| Send to: | Heartsong Presents Reader's Service |
| --- | --- |
| | P.O. Box 719 |
| | Uhrichsville, Ohio 44683 |

Please send me ____ copies of *Christmas Treasures*. I am
enclosing **$4.97 each** (please add $1.00 to cover postage and
handling per order. OH add 6.25% tax. NJ add 6% tax.). Send
check or money order, no cash or C.O.D.s, please.
  **To place a credit card order, call 1-800-847-8270.**

NAME _____

ADDRESS _____

CITY/STATE _____ ZIP _____

# ······ Hearts♥ng ······

## HISTORICAL ROMANCE IS CHEAPER BY THE DOZEN!

**Any 12 *Heartsong Presents* titles for only $26.95** **

**Buy any assortment of twelve *Heartsong Presents* titles and save 25% off of the already discounted price of $2.95 each!**

**plus $1.00 shipping and handling per order and sales tax where applicable.

### HEARTSONG PRESENTS TITLES AVAILABLE NOW:

__HP 28   DAKOTA DAWN, *Lauraine Snelling*
__HP 40   PERFECT LOVE, *Janelle Jamison*
__HP 43   VEILED JOY, *Colleen L. Reece*
__HP 44   DAKOTA DREAM, *Lauraine Snelling*
__HP 51   THE UNFOLDING HEART, *JoAnn A. Grote*
__HP 55   TREASURE OF THE HEART, *JoAnn A. Grote*
__HP 56   A LIGHT IN THE WINDOW, *Janelle Jamison*
__HP 59   EYES OF THE HEART, *Maryn Langer*
__HP 60   MORE THAN CONQUERORS, *Kay Cornelius*
__HP 63   THE WILLING HEART, *Janelle Jamison*
__HP 64   CROWS'-NESTS AND MIRRORS, *Colleen L. Reece*
__HP 67   DAKOTA DUSK, *Lauraine Snelling*
__HP 68   RIVERS RUSHING TO THE SEA, *Jacquelyn Cook*
__HP 71   DESTINY'S ROAD, *Janelle Jamison*
__HP 72   SONG OF CAPTIVITY, *Linda Herring*
__HP 75   MUSIC IN THE MOUNTAINS, *Colleen L. Reece*
__HP 76   HEARTBREAK TRAIL, *VeraLee Wiggins*
__HP 87   SIGN OF THE BOW, *Kay Cornelius*
__HP 88   BEYOND TODAY, *Janelle Jamison*
__HP 91   SIGN OF THE EAGLE, *Kay Cornelius*
__HP 92   ABRAM MY LOVE, *VeraLee Wiggins*
__HP 95   SIGN OF THE DOVE, *Kay Cornelius*
__HP 96   FLOWER OF SEATTLE, *Colleen L. Reece*
__HP 99   ANOTHER TIME...ANOTHER PLACE, *Bonnie L. Crank*
__HP100   RIVER OF PEACE, *Janelle Burnham*
__HP103   LOVE'S SHINING HOPE, *JoAnn A. Grote*
__HP104   HAVEN OF PEACE, *Carol Mason Parker*
__HP107   PIONEER LEGACY, *Norene Morris*
__HP111   A KINGDOM DIVIDED, *Tracie J. Peterson*
__HP112   CAPTIVES OF THE CANYON, *Colleen L. Reece*
__HP115   SISTERS IN THE SUN, *Shirley Rhode*
__HP116   THE HEART'S CALLING, *Tracie J. Peterson*
__HP119   BECKONING STREAMS, *Janelle Burnham*
__HP120   AN HONEST LOVE, *JoAnn A. Grote*
__HP123   THE HEART HAS ITS REASONS, *Birdie L. Etchison*
__HP124   HIS NAME ON HER HEART, *Mary LaPietra*
__HP127   FOREVER YOURS, *Tracie J. Peterson*
__HP128   MISPLACED ANGEL, *VeraLee Wiggins*
__HP131   LOVE IN THE PRAIRIE WILDS, *Robin Chandler*
__HP132   LOST CREEK MISSION, *Cheryl Tenbrook*

(If ordering from this page, please remember to include it with the order form.)

# ···········Presents ········

## Great Inspirational Romance at a Great Price!

**Heartsong Presents** books are inspirational romances in contemporary and historical settings, designed to give you an enjoyable, spirit-lifting reading experience. You can choose wonderfully written titles from some of today's best authors like Peggy Darty, Colleen L. Reece, Tracie J. Peterson, VeraLee Wiggins, and many others.

*When ordering quantities less than twelve, above titles are $2.95 each.*

---

SEND TO: Heartsong Presents Reader's Service
P.O. Box 719, Uhrichsville, Ohio 44683

Please send me the items checked above. I am enclosing $_____.
(please add $1.00 to cover postage per order. OH add 6.25% tax. NJ add 6%). Send check or money order, no cash or C.O.Ds, please.
**To place a credit card order, call 1-800-847-8270.**

NAME _____

ADDRESS _____

CITY/STATE_____ ZIP _____

# Heartsong Presents
# *Love Stories Are Rated G!*

That's for godly, gratifying, and of course, great! If you love a thrilling love story, but don't appreciate the sordidness of some popular paperback romances, **Heartsong Presents** is for you. In fact, **Heartsong Presents** is the *only inspirational romance book club*, the only one featuring love stories where Christian faith is the primary ingredient in a marriage relationship.

Sign up today to receive your first set of four, never before published Christian romances. Send no money now; you will receive a bill with the first shipment. You may cancel at any time without obligation, and if you aren't completely satisfied with any selection, you may return the books for an immediate refund!

Imagine. . .four new romances every four weeks—two historical, two contemporary—with men and women like you who long to meet the one God has chosen as the love of their lives. . .all for the low price of $9.97 postpaid.

*To join, simply complete the coupon below and mail to the address provided.* **Heartsong Presents** romances are rated G for another reason: They'll arrive *Godspeed!*

## YES! Sign me up for Heartsong!

**NEW MEMBERSHIPS WILL BE SHIPPED IMMEDIATELY!**
**Send no money now.** We'll bill you only $9.97 post-paid with your first shipment of four books. Or for faster action, call toll free 1-800-847-8270.

NAME _____

ADDRESS _____

CITY _____ STATE _____ ZIP _____

**MAIL TO:** HEARTSONG PRESENTS, P.O. Box 719, Uhrichsville, Ohio 44683

YES10-96